My Bigfoot Boyfriend

VALERIE LOVELESS

To my human family.

Prologue

The heavy footsteps thudded behind her, so closely that she could feel the vibration through the ground, working its way up her limbs. She could feel her heartbeat in her ears as she ran. She picked up the pace as best she could but with the dense trees, dripping with green mosses and wet from a recent snow melt, it was not easy going. Felicity's heart pumped with a ferocity for survival as she went tearing through small branches, some scraping and abrading her. Her face was wet with perspiration and her shoes were soaked through from the puddles she had trod through. If only she could stop for a moment to catch her breath, but the heavy footsteps still pursued her. She didn't know where she was going, only that she had to get away.

She went to jump over a fallen log, but she miscalculated, and her back leg caught the top of it which sent her face forward, toward the dark, wet, forest floor. She tried to catch herself, but her arms couldn't move fast enough and only one elbow was able to stop her fall. This painfully wrenched her shoulder and most of her face hit the spongy ground except for her forehead which landed on a broken branch and split her forehead. Instantly her world went black and she no longer cared about running from her pursuer.

Chapter One

As Felicity headed down the winding road in southern Washington, her thoughts were ever turning to her dead uncle. She swerved her old gray civic gently around a massive tree that had taken over half the lane. She turned up her wipers as the mist turned to sprinkles, impairing her vision.

"What the crap!" She yelled to no one. "Doesn't anyone maintain this road?" *She wasn't that far from civilization.* The cabin her uncle had left her was supposed to only be about fifteen miles from the nearest town. However, the nearest town was a small, piddly place that was about twenty-five miles from the nearest city and up here in the Pacific Northwest, everything seemed thousands of miles apart. There was little between landmarks that was discernible. It was mostly heavy, old growth forest.

Felicity's uncle Ben had left her his little hunting cabin in Eatonville after he passed six months ago. Well, it wasn't exactly Eatonville, but that was the nearest town to the cabin. She didn't actually know her uncle Ben, but apparently, she was the only family left that he didn't hate. She recalled meeting him once or twice when she was little, but other than that, she never heard from him. Occasionally, her mom would mention that she had fought with her brother, Uncle Ben again, but it was never clear what they fought about or why.

Since Felicity had just quit her job as a successful marketer, due to a near mental breakdown, she thought it might be a great time to venture out of her typical life and try vacation rentals. She had this free cabin her uncle gave her, why not start there? Even though she had never seen it before, she had a plan to fix up the place and rent it as a B&B. Her father had been to the cabin with Uncle Ben once, and he had said it was a decent size. She prodded him for more details, like how many bedrooms, how many baths? He seemed to remember it had three bedrooms and two bathrooms.

Felicity's heart jumped again as she saw another tree in the road. This time right in the middle of the lane. She slammed on the brakes, intending to swerve but the tree suddenly bounded off to the left. "What the crap! What the? What the actual crap!" She shuddered as she swerved and craned her neck around to see where the tree had gone. By now she was fairly certain it wasn't a tree. What could it be? It was so massive, it had to have been ten, no- twelve feet tall. Then, as she looked in her rear-view mirror, she saw the massive form run into the tree line on two man-like legs. She could even see fur fluttering off of its arms as it strode off. Could it have been a bear? They stood upright sometimes... It was too tall to be a man and too swift to have been a bumbling bear on its hindlegs.

What then could it have been?

Felicity wasn't keen on worrying about such things and she took a deep breath and let the memory fade quickly as she pressed on to the cabin. Her GPS interrupted her thoughts, *"You should arrive at your destination at nine-seventeen PM."*

The last remaining miles passed as slowly as all the rest. As she pulled up to where the GPS told her to pull off, she could see no road. She hesitated to get out, but she couldn't see where she should turn. There were only brambles and bushes as far as she could see. "Ok, you can do this. If you see another bear man you can just jump back in your car and drive all the way back to California," she told herself as she opened the door to her car and pulled the hood to her raincoat over her head. She walked as far as she could before there was nothing but bushes. There was nothing there! She walked back and forth at the spot a few times and finally she noticed a glint of metal. She inspected it further using her phone flashlight. It was a chain. Ah, a gate. The gate had been overgrown by the vegetation and it made a spectacular camouflage for the entrance to a secret hunting cabin.

A car drove by as she fiddled with the gate. It gave a few friendly beeps to the horn. Felicity awkwardly waved as she pulled on the chain. It was placed over the pole and through the gate to loosely hold it shut, once the chain was off, it easily swung open, taking a few bits of the bushes with it. Felicity hopped back into her car and drove through heading carefully down the narrow lane. The sprinkling had turned to medium rainfall and the headlights mixed with the darkness of the night and the denseness of the forest made it difficult to see. Felicity pressed on. The driveway was longer than she expected. So long, in fact, she wondered if she would ever make it to the cabin. It was full of potholes and dips and her little car bottomed out many times. Finally, a clearing appeared and at the back of the clearing was Uncle Ben's cabin. It looked much like you'd expect a cabin to look. It was made of logs and had a green metal roof that was steeply pitched. There appeared to be a second floor with dormer windows that faced the front of the house. Moss was dripping off the front porch and on the corners of the roof. The clearing was littered with logs and branches, probably from whatever storm had recently come through this area.

She pulled her car into the middle of the clearing and prepared herself for what she might find inside. She wasn't sure what state the cabin would be in, so she came prepared. She figured no matter what, she would be able to pitch a tent in the middle of the cabin. Even if it didn't have a roof the tent would provide shelter for her, but the roof looked to be in good condition, so she was less worried.

As far as she knew, her uncle had used the cabin up until a year ago, when he ended up in the hospital on his deathbed. It took the lawyers that long to get his affairs settled and let her know that she had inherited the property. Her mother and father were jealous but not surprised by it. Uncle Ben had threatened to disinherit them many times. Her mom was the youngest and Uncle Ben was the oldest of the family, so they weren't particularly close being so far apart in age. It didn't help that her mom was from a second wife, which made them only half siblings.

Felicity exited her car and looked around. It was darker here than she was used to. There were no streetlights, city lights or vehicle lights. She popped open the trunk and grabbed her backpack and the tent. She searched about her pocket for the key that the lawyer had given her that hopefully was for the front door. Felicity hit the lock button on her key fob and the headlights to her vehicle turned off drowning her in a sea of misty, wet, blackness. As her shoes crunched on the spongy, gravel covered ground, she looked up at the sky. In the city, the sky was the darkest thing at night. Here, the sky was brighter as it was lit up with a spray of billions of stars like she had never seen before. There was no moon, just the ominous, towering presence of trees and countless, new star friends.

She had never felt so alone.

She took out her phone and turned on the flashlight app as she carefully made her way to the front door, stepping over logs and tufts of grass as she went.

She stopped for a moment as she walked up the steps. She thought she heard a rustling in the woods to her left. She shone her mobile phone flashlight into the tree line, but she saw nothing except for the occasional rain drop streaking like a comet in the night sky. She shuddered and whispered to herself, "What the crap am I doing? What kind of a dummy am I? Coming out here in the middle of the night, to the middle of nowhere! All alone! Not that I would have anyone to bring with me anyway…"

As quickly as she could, Felicity tried to unlock the front door, but it became clear that this was not the right key. The hairs on the back of her neck began to raise. The sounds of the rain intensified like tiny monsters coming to get her and a million questions and thoughts swirled through her mind: *Was this not the right cabin? Perhaps he had given her the wrong key? Was it Washington state? What if it was Washington DC? Are there cabins in Washington DC? It had to be Washington state.*

The GPS recognized the address, it had to be this cabin, but what if someone had taken over this cabin since her uncle's been gone? What if they claimed it for their own... and they were an axe murderer? Were they inside waiting for some witless girl to come along to become their prey? Maybe they would send her out into the woods, naked, with bells on while they chased her down and hunted her with a crossbow— Or maybe there was another door that this key went to. A side door or a backdoor? The thought of a backdoor or a side door was just as freaky as the axe murderer. While the front of the cabin faced the clearing and seemed safe because she could see if something was coming towards her, the sides and the back were very close to the tree line. Their density could conceal anyone, or anything. Steadying herself before she went, Felicity walked to the side of the porch and peeked her head around. There was no door, so she walked to the other side. She found a door with clearly placed steppingstones leading towards it. Felicity prayed that the key would work.

    She thought about hopping over the top of the porch rail, but when she put her hand on the rail to do it, it was wet and slimy with moss that seemed to be dripping off of every horizontal surface in the forest. Instead, she walked down the steps of the front porch and walked around. There was only a small lean-to with a few scant pieces of wood inside and a side door. Again, she thought she heard a scratching noise in the tree line behind her. She hoped it was just wind rustling a few branches, or a squirrel jumping from tree to tree. She scrambled to get the key into the keyhole. This time the key satisfactorily engaged with the lock and turned the tumbler easily, the dead bolt resisted only slightly as it disengaged from the jamb. The door swung open freely as she cast the light of her phone into the empty room, the cabin had been empty for quite some time and the illuminated dust floating through the air made the cabin look misty and mysterious.

    Felicity heard a rustling in the woods right behind her that made her heart nearly stop. She wasn't interested in waiting around to see if something would come out and greet her or not, so she took her chances and stepped into the cabin and quickly shut the door behind her turning the deadbolt.

    She was standing in a small rustic kitchen. "Lights?" Oh, how she prayed that there was electricity in this place, what a long night it would be if she could not turn on the lights.

    Felicity had spent some time going through old abandoned homes. As a marketer she would help real estate agents sell old "charming" homes. Those homes often had a strange and forgotten smell of stagnant pipes and empty dreams. The cabin didn't smell like any of those things. If anything, it smelled wonderful. Like pine, fresh rain and gun oil.

    Felicity spotted a light switch near the door. Now blessed by photons to excite her eyeballs, she looked around at her surroundings. The kitchen had dark brown cabinets with rustic iron handles on the doors and drawers. The countertops were a dark brown butcher block that matched the plaid curtains hanging in the kitchen window. "Not bad Uncle Ben. I expected something a bit less homey." The floors were dark stained pine wood and there was a nineteen-sixties table with chrome legs and the sparkling yellow melamine top with matching yellow vinyl chairs. All very dated but still charming.

Felicity made her way through the kitchen to the living room. This room had a vaulted ceiling with stairs to the left that went up to the loft, and a hallway that went down underneath the loft. There was a yellow couch with an old-fashioned daisy pattern and an old red, oriental rug on the floor. Uncle Ben must have been a great marksman because there were several deer heads hanging on the walls and one jackalope, a made-up animal made out of a rabbit head with small antlers attached to it. She remembered her father joking about a jackalope.

Felicity found another switch that turned on a chandelier hanging from the second story of the vaulted ceiling that was made out of antlers. She began to feel hopeful that she would not have to sleep in her tent in a sleeping bag tonight.

Where to go next? The loft or down the hallway? "I think I'll try upstairs," she headed up the small staircase. It turned out the loft was no more than a large room with steeply pitched walls. There was a comfortable looking bed on one wall, an old-fashioned dresser next to it and at the end of the bed was an old army footlocker. Felicity made a note to open that up and go through its contents later. She headed back downstairs and down the hallway where there were several doors. The first door was the bathroom. She peeked inside, more yellow. At least the tub and sink were white porcelain, she had seen yellow fixtures before, and it was horrific. Then she headed down to the next door which was a bedroom that was full of bunk beds. The small room could have slept six people easily which made Felicity excited by the rental possibilities. The next two rooms had queen size beds in each. In the last room at the end of the hall, it appeared to be what most people would call a master bedroom as it had a private bathroom with a shower and thank goodness, none of it was yellow. The bed appeared to be a king size bed made out of giant logs. Everything in the cabin seemed to be tidy if not a bit dusty, not as dusty as Felicity would have expected.

Dropping her bag on the chair next to the bed, she checked out the covers and the sheets just in case there were any critters who had taken up home there while the cabin was empty. She turned out the lights and plopped into the bed. It was a bit hard; her uncle Ben must have had some aversion to a comfy bed or was too cheap to get a decent mattress.

Felicity rolled over and looked out the window across the room, she could have sworn she saw movement, but it was raining so she tried to think little of it. She turned her thoughts to the life she had left behind. Even though she was alone, in a strange town and a strange bed, she didn't regret leaving- at all. She felt hopeful and satisfied that this could be the beginning of a simpler, more wholesome life for her. A bit of movement caught her eye again, and she saw the whites of a pair of eyes looking right at her. Her breath caught in her throat as the fear paralyzed her. The eyes closed and disappeared. "Please be a wild animal and not that hulking creature I saw on the road," she whispered to herself, but she knew that whatever was looking in would have to be very tall to see in the windows, even on the main floor.

It was a long and sleepless night as she tried and failed to relax. She knew she had heard rustling in the woods, she knew she had seen a large monster on the road and now something was watching her.

Forget a B&B! I am leaving first thing in the morning, she thought. *This is more than I can take.*

As she lay there on the large dusty bed her thoughts turned to Lan. Lancaster. Lancaster Kennedy. She hadn't thought about him in forever. He was the cutest boy in eighth grade. He had big blue eyes and long lashes that were set in a frame of dark wavy hair. He was cute all the way through high school, too. But he was so shy, and he always had a girlfriend. But there was that one time he talked to her. He asked her what classes she had next and even walked with her talking about how cool the science teacher was until they parted ways. Looking back, with that good ol' twenty-twenty hindsight she could see that he was flirting with her, but she was too dumb to see it then. She had always thought she didn't have a chance with him, but she did have that one fleeting moment and she squandered it by being shy. Her mind began to mingle her memories with dreams and the next thing she knew it was morning.

As the sun came up, Felicity dared to venture from the bedroom she was in. She had a perhaps unfounded fear, that whatever was outside looking in had come in during the night.

So, she tiptoed through the cabin and into the kitchen. Everything looked so cozy and homey in the daylight. Even the sun shone through the windows this morning. She had not seen the sun since before she drove through Oregon. She grabbed her bag and went to leave through the kitchen, but she saw a pair of keys hanging on a nail near the light switch. She grabbed them, hoping it was for the front door, and if she ever did have to come back to this place, she would use the front door like a sensible scaredy-cat.

She hopped in her car and took off at a speed that said she was never coming back to this place.

The drive was much more pleasant in the morning. It was like a movie set in the woods. They didn't have lush and green forests where she was from, they were dry and sparse and mostly piñon pines. Here, the redwoods and pines towered and dripped with constant moisture and moss. It reminded her of the movie Star Wars that she used to watch with her high school sweetheart David. What a nerd he was. But he was so sweet. Felicity, however, wasn't interested in sweetness at that time and dumped him for the guy with the homemade tattoo of a snake on his forearm. Of course, 'tattoo guy' wasn't interested in Felicity because she was too pure and they never got together and by the time she realized it was never going to happen, David had a new girlfriend, Sophie, whom he ended up marrying. Felicity regretted those actions a lot, especially when she perused his Facebook and saw what a wonderful life they had built together with a home, a few kids and lots of travel. Felicity was still single and hadn't even had a boyfriend for— she lost count how many years.

    As she arrived into town, she decided she could use some gas and breakfast before heading back to California, and perhaps she should consider getting a hotel room. She pulled into an old looking gas station near an even older looking diner.

    It was a crisp morning and the sun had barely come up due to the height of the trees in the area. The diner looked like an old train car covered in graffiti. It was situated right off of the road. A nice-looking man in a leather jacket opened the door for her.

"Morning ma'am."

"Morning, thank you." She nodded and smiled as she walked over to the counter and sat down on the old wooden stool. The place smelled of frying oil and fruit pie. Not a bad combination. A young girl in a dirty, white shirt and jeans, of about fifteen came over with a pad and pen.

"What can I get for you?" She said, head bobbing slightly with attitude.

"I don't know, I'm new here. What's good?"

"Well, we are known for pie." she gestured toward the door to a fluorescent sign that said, "*World's best pie!*"

"I'm not much of a 'pie for breakfast' person, I'm afraid."

"Well, then how about just pancakes and eggs?"

Felicity nodded. "Bacon on the side?"

"K!" The girl walked toward the kitchen and slapped the note paper on the counter between the kitchen and the register area.

The nice-looking man that held the door open for her came and sat next to her.

"You mind if I join you?"

"Oh, I guess not." Felicity smiled timidly. She wasn't used to strangers being so friendly.

"I'm Connor. Are you from around here?"

"My uncle left me his cabin down the road, I'm Felicity."

"Oh, Ben? I think I saw you last night trying to get in his gate. I gave the horn a pop. I'm sorry for your loss, Ben was a friend of mine."

"Thank you. Honestly, I barely knew him, so I guess the condolences are mine to give."

"Oh, thanks. How'd you wind up with his cabin then? It's a nice piece of real estate."

"I guess I was the only family he had left that he didn't hate."

"Nice. Sounds like Ben."

Felicity nodded and swallowed hard before she said, "So you live around here?" Connor nodded and took a drink of his coffee. He had nice eyes and a kind smile, but he seemed a few years too old for Felicity, especially now that she knew he was Uncle Ben's friend.

"Yeah. I'm just a few cabins down from you. Hey, if you ever need anything let me know."

"Oh, you taking off?"

"No, not until I get my pie."

"Oh, morning pie huh?"

"Yep, keeps me going all day." Connor laughed.

"Can I ask you something?" She didn't wait for him to answer, and he leaned in conspiratorially, "Are there any suspicious people, or say— creatures that I should be aware of?"

"Like what? You mean bears? Or cougars?" He leaned back.

"Yeah, really big ones?"

"Naw, just regular size. In fact, we don't really even have any around here. Too many hunters."

"Oh, I wonder what I saw then."

"What did it look like?"

"I saw something on the side of the road the other night. Something huge on two legs. Had to have been a bear, right?"

"Ah! Yeah, now I know what you mean. I don't want to scare you but, there have been some sightings."

"Of bears?"

"No, no. Not exactly."

"What else could it possibly be? Whatever it was, I think it was looking in my window last night too."

Connor leaned in close and whispered, "Bigfoot."

"Bigfoot?" Felicity replied too loudly.

The young waitress came back with a plate, "you've seen it too?" She set her plate down roughly.

"I don't know what I saw. I didn't think Bigfoot was real."

"I've seen it *bunches* of times. I think there's a whole family."

"Of Bigfeet?"

"Bigfoots" the waitress corrected. "Bigfoot is a proper noun; therefore, you don't change the spelling to the plural for foot," She then air quoted, "'feet'. You just add an 'S' to make it plural." Felicity was surprised that the same aloof girl who took her order several minutes ago suddenly awoke with knowledge and wisdom.

An older gentleman sitting in a booth behind her chimed in.

"Where I'm from we call 'em the skunk ape, they are real nasty smelling. I saw one down the road a few weeks ago. Just standing there, like he was hitching for a ride."

Connor put his hands up, "Okay everyone, let's not scare the new girl in town."

"I'm not really sure what to think now. Everyone seems so certain that it exists, and if I hadn't seen what I saw last night I might think you're all crazy. Is it dangerous?"

They all answered at the same time. "No."

"Well," the old man countered, "I wouldn't be out in the woods by myself after dark if I were you."

"I've never heard of anyone getting hurt, but I've never heard of it looking in anyone's windows either." Connor admitted as the waitress brought him his pie. He took a bite immediately.

"Interesting." The little waitress mused. "It shows signs of intelligence and awareness."

"Course it does!" the old man barked. "They are the missing link; they are darn near human."

"I'm afraid to go back to the cabin." Felicity admitted.

"That's smart." The old man said.

"Now, hold on!" Connor said through a full mouth of pie. "I've lived here my whole life and I've never heard of it hurting no one."

"Are you sure? I'm all alone."

"Listen," the waitress said after popping her gum. "Connor's right. It's scary to think that a big hairy man is out there watching your every move but like, nobody's ever really been hurt. So statistically, you should be, like, fine." The waitress set Felicity's plate in front of her, the bacon was still sizzling.

"I really need to get the place fixed up so I can rent it out. I don't suppose having a Bigfoot in your backyard is a big selling point around here?"

Connor laughed. Felicity ate a bite of her eggs and then followed it with a buttery pancake that she doused in blueberry syrup. The diner went back to the soundtrack from grease playing quietly in the background. She had a flashback to a time her mom and dad took her to a similar looking joint after her graduation. They had lectured her about not making plans for college and how she needed to stop dreaming and make a choice about her life. So, she did. Little good it did her though. She still wasn't happy. She had accomplished all the goals they had made for her that day; undergrad, masters, internship and then marketing professional, but she felt empty and unfulfilled. Perhaps it was because it was their dream for her to go to college and have a career that left her with no time for a life, and not hers.

After a good breakfast and filling up the car with gas, Felicity got back on the road. She considered driving back to California. She weighed her options. She could go home and hire someone to sell the place, or she could "man up" and go back. She could fix the place up herself and live like someone on a reality show about a single woman who runs a cabin B&B in the woods of Washington state that is being stalked by an upright walking bear… Still not convinced in the existence of Bigfoot. All internal joking aside, she had no job to go back to anymore. She quit. She had nothing to lose, and it could be a fun adventure. Or a nightmare. Maybe she could write a book about it. A memoir, *or* she could actually pitch it to HGTV. It could be called *Bigfoot Cabin* and she could wear belted muumuus all of the time and cook people roadkill for breakfast. Her thoughts had gotten away with her and before she realized it, she was driving back to her inheritance.

She slammed on her breaks, not because she saw another monster but because she drove right past the entrance to the driveway. Someone had shut the gate.

"So, this thing is a good Samaritan now?" then she considered, it could have just been Connor being a good neighbor, or any neighbor really. She begrudgingly got out and re-opened the gate intending for it to stay open. "Leave my gate alone!" She yelled to her Bigfoot, or bear, or nosy neighbor.

She drove down the drive back into the clearing. Putting the car in park she looked around. Nothing looked as though it had been disturbed. So, she carefully got out of the car, being ever vigilant of her surroundings. She got her key ready for what she hoped was to the front door. She walked quickly but quietly. The key easily slid in the lock and turned so she let herself in and locked the deadbolt behind her.

She looked around the house again. It was so quiet here. Not a street sound, not even a chirping bird outside. She held as still as possible so that she could hear if there was someone or *something* in the cabin.

After what felt like an eternity, and nearly blacking out from holding her breath, she decided she was alone. After wandering around the cabin in the daytime, taking it all in, she thought she should get to work with cleaning and organizing.

Her mom was an OCD clean freak. While Felicity did not follow in her footsteps, she certainly knew a dirty place when she saw one. Her mother always told her that people would 'hide their filth with tidiness'. That having everything in place did not mean it was clean, just picked up. Her mom often took cleanliness so far that she wouldn't even allow someone to walk across the carpet with dirty shoes in their hands for fear the germs and dirt could invisibly drip off as you went. Felicity would purposely walk across the carpet with shoes on when she was a teen just to spite her mother, but only when she was not looking. The one time her mother did see her do it, she had to spend the evening cleaning the carpet. Even though her mom was the *freak* of clean freaks, she was loving. She and Felicity had a lasting, good friendship.

She found a closet with cleaning supplies inside; it was also stocked with lightbulbs. She went around the house checking all the lights, dusting the fixtures, and wiping down every flat surface. She found the cabin had a laundry room, so she started stripping the bedding off and washing all the linens and towels. She cleaned all day, scrubbing corners and swabbing window tracks, until it began to get dark. For the most part, she had forgotten about her Bigfoot stalker. Now that it was dark, she felt very alone. Every moment the sky became drenched in more inky blackness, the more she became full of fear. She kept repeating to herself what those in the diner told her; that he had never hurt anybody, and she would be fine.

She decided that if she turned on the TV perhaps, she would feel less alone and frightened. So, she snuggled up in a blanket she found in the linen closet and watched Wheel of Fortune. There were few channels that came through on the old tv, even though it had a digital converter box. She made a mental note that she would need to get a satellite dish for this place.

Eventually she snoozed off with all the lights left on. Lulled by the dulcet tones of the late-night talk shows, she awoke to the sound of an annoying local commercial about bail bonds and realized that the cabin was freezing. She looked outside and saw that it had started snowing.

"Hmm, I didn't think that it snowed here." It was February after all. Then, Felicity heard a loud banging sound. She turned down the TV and listened more intently. Again, and again the banging came, then a louder bang, clearly against the cabin itself made her jump out of her skin! "He's never hurt anyone before!" She told herself again. She crawled to the window and peeked out. She couldn't see anything except the dark silhouettes of trees covered in snow. She crept to the kitchen and carefully spied out that window. Nothing. Then all the lights went out. In fact, the electricity in the entire cabin went out. "He's never hurt anyone before." She whispered to herself again.

Maybe she could make a run for it to her car. She looked out at her little gray civic buried in snow. It would likely not make it down the driveway. She imagined the little tires spinning out and flinging snow and mud. Thud, thud, thud. Heavy footsteps tread through the snow. Should she call out? What if it was just Connor, here to help with the electricity. But, how would he have known? And the banging outside before? The footsteps stopped and she could hear heavy logs being tossed about. Oh, Good. It was just Connor, he brought her some firewood. She stood cautiously and looked out the kitchen window more relaxed than before.

She couldn't see it clearly, but she saw enough. A huge, hairy creature stood on two legs like a man, just beyond the window and several feet from the door. It faced away from the window. She watched as it appeared to rip a log in two with its bare hands and toss the two pieces into a pile. Then it went out of view, returning shortly to stack wood under the storage shed.

It appeared to be naked but covered completely in hair that seemed too long for a bear. It turned towards the window and Felicity ducked. As she crouched and shivered, she swore she could see her breath. Had this creature made the cabin cold inside like one of those ghost stories she had read on one of her lonely nights at home after work? In the stories, just before the haunting manifested the haunted would see their breath condensing before them, when just before the room was a perfectly normal temperature. Could this be some paranormal creature? She only knew one thing for certain. Bears don't cut, rip and stack firewood.

The heavy footsteps started again but they disappeared into the night.

Felicity stayed in her hiding place until she could no longer squat down and the cold of the night became too much to bear. How had it gotten so cold so fast? It was a nice day yesterday, a little chilly but certainly not *snowy* weather. Of course, as a California girl, anything under seventy felt like an ice storm to her. She pawed around for her phone in the darkness and after stubbing her toe several times, she found it on the couch. She turned on the phone's flashlight and went to find the breaker box. She seemed to remember it was near the linen closet in the hallway. She was right. She opened it.

She knew very little about electricity, but she knew that if one of the breakers was a different direction than the rest, that it had flipped and cut off the power. None of the breakers were flipped. She tried them all, anyway, flipping the heavy switches back and forth. Nothing. She would succumb to the terrible cold if she did not find a way to heat this place!

There was a cast iron stove in the living room, but she didn't have any wood. No. Wait, that wasn't true. That Bigfoot did seem to be stacking wood in the shed. Did she dare go outside? What if it was a trap? What if the creature knew she would be freezing and would need firewood? Haplessly she would be lulled outside by the temptation of a warm fire and then when her arms were full of a heavy load of wood- that's when it would Bigfoot-nap her! There was no other heat in the cabin, with or without the electricity other than the stove. She had no choice.

She unlocked the door as quietly as humanly possible. The deadbolt fell heavily against the inner casing of the lock, making Felicity wince. She opened the door slowly, just a crack and popped her head out casing out the side yard. She stepped onto the ground and yelped as her barefoot stepped on fresh, freezing cold snow. No going back now! She leapt over to the woodshed, taking as big of steps as possible to avoid touching the snow with her feet. She grabbed as many pieces as she could. Something on top of the shed caught her attention. The roof was low, maybe forty-eight inches and on top of it was a box. She looked at it more carefully, it was a box of matches. Was that there before? It wasn't covered in snow so the Bigfoot must have placed it there. She grabbed it and leapt, much less gracefully due to her arms being full of wood, back into the cabin.

"Oh my gosh, oh my gosh!" She cried as she shook off her wet, frozen feet. She stomped into the living room and dropped the wood next to the stove. She hoped she could figure out how to start a fire now. She had a general idea. She needed something that burned easily to start it and then she could pile larger wood on top. Luckily, she had matches.

She found a pile of old newspapers and magazines in a box near the stove and began crumpling and shoving it into the oven. Then she placed a single log into the stove. It didn't catch so she kept shoving more and more paper into the stove until, eureka! It finally caught. Then she put another log on the fire. Within minutes the whole cabin was beginning to warm up. She could no longer see her breath and even her red and pulsing toes began to feel normal again.

Why would a Bigfoot have or leave matches? She began to second guess what she had seen. But there was no denying that she saw a hulking, fully covered in hair creature!

She settled back onto the couch and just when she thought she would fall into a coma of warm sleep, she heard a frighteningly, other worldly howl. Her eyes popped nearly from her head as she sat up like a board. It didn't sound like a wolf... Not that she had ever heard a wolf in real life, but she *knew* it wasn't a dog. It was like nothing she had ever heard before. A chill flew down her spine and she hid her head in the blanket until an uneasy sleep took her.

The next morning Felicity woke to the brightness of a new day. Snow glistened in her windows. The cabin had gotten cold again as she did not maintain the fire through the night. But it was still glowing with some embers and so she threw in another log and a few pieces of paper and hoped it would start up again. She thought she might attempt to venture out to the diner again for breakfast as she still had not stocked anything at the house. She checked the lights and they still would not turn on.

Perhaps Connor could be of some assistance in this regard and he was the only person she really knew. Or at least she knew his name and that he knew Uncle Ben. How would she tell him that the Bigfoot cut her power and then gave her firewood?

After dressing without taking a shower, since she figured there would be no hot water, Felicity tramped through the snow to her little car. It was well covered in about eight inches of snow. So was the driveway, there was no way she would be able to get out and she was starving. Maybe it wouldn't be as bad as she thought. She just needed to get down the drive and then the road would probably be cleared. She cleaned off the windshield with her sleeve and then got inside. The car had a little trouble starting, but it did. She let it run for a few minutes with the heater running because the steering wheel was too uncomfortably cold to touch.

"Alright baby! Let's get out of here. Momma's hungry!" She put her foot on the gas and the car didn't move an inch. "Shoot!" She tried again, a little harder this time. Nothing but spinning wheels. Then she pumped the gas and the car rocked a little but still did not move. She tried again and again, the wheels spinning and the engine loudly revving. Nothing but a slight fishtailing with no forward momentum.

Getting out of the car, she swore, "damn, I'm going to starve out here!" She slammed the door shut and ran back into the cabin.

She rifled through the kitchen cupboards. There was nothing of substance, just basics like salt and pepper. She did find a pack of gum that was hard as rocks. It still tasted good and after sucking on it for a while it did soften to a chewable state.

Then a thought occurred to her. She could call for help. Maybe AAA could come pull her out of the driveway or maybe the diner delivered? It was a long shot but, duh! She had a phone; she wasn't stranded necessarily. Maybe the diner could give her Connor's phone number. She knew a guy like him would have a truck with four-wheel drive. She could just tell.

She pulled up the map on her phone and found the diner easily: Caboose your Moose Train Car Diner. When she tapped the name of the diner it pulled up the info including the number.

"Hey, hi. Um. I'm Ben Hackett's niece. Oh, you don't know who that is? Well he died a few months ago. Yes, thank you for your kind words, so you do know him? Oh. I see well thank you for being kind even though you didn't know him. Anyway. I'm stranded up here at the house, I mean cabin and um, I was wondering if you knew Connor's number so I could call for help. He's a regular there. He's like thirty to forty-five years, brownish hair, he's a man, I guess you could have figured since I said he… like average height. Yeah, that's like a lot of people isn't it… Well, he eats pie for breakfast and—oh he's there? Great! Can I talk to—Connor, hi! It's Felicity. Yeah, Ben's niece. Listen—oh yeah, I'd love some pie, that's actually why I'm calling, because I am stuck at the cabin in the snow, and I was wondering if you had a way to pull me out? You can? Oh, not until this evening. No, it's not an emergency I just can't get out. No please, don't worry it can wait until this evening." Felicity looked down at the package of gum. Her one form of sustenance for the whole day and frowned. "Thank you so much Connor. I really appreciate it. Okay, see you tonight."

    Felicity sat on the yellow floral couch and sighed. Why did she have to be such a pushover? She could have told him she was starving and maybe he could have made it work. But what an imposition she would have put him in for him to leave work and come help her. She wouldn't starve. Not in one day. She probably had some dehydrated french fries under her car seat. She'd be fine. The big problem was starving her mind. No electricity. Her phone would be dead in a few hours if she didn't shut it off. There was no tv, no radio. She could sit in her car and listen to the radio for a few hours and charge her phone, she'd likely fall asleep though. Radio was no fun if you weren't otherwise occupied. Apparently, Uncle Ben couldn't read because there wasn't a single book in the whole cabin and Felicity had gifted or donated all of her books when she left so she could "travel light". That's what she told her mom when she handed over a box of her favorite Jane Austen's and a few classics she had picked up in college that she was *never* going to read again.

    The cabin was spotless. There was little she could do. She could explore outside… But there was that thing out there. Probably watching her every move. Then she remembered the footlocker up in the loft. Hopefully there would be some treasures in there. Why else would you keep a footlocker at the end of a bed.

Chapter Two

It only had extra bedding in it.

"Ugh! I'm going to die of boredom!" She said as she fell on the bed. She had a great view from the bed of the surrounding woods. There was some movement, so she got up and went closer to the window. A deer probably. No, too big.

It was moving through the trees, so she never got a full view of it, but she soon realized what she was seeing, and it was coming straight for her and she realized that she hadn't locked the front door.

"Oh my gosh!" She shrieked as she bounded down the stairs and fell at the front door just in time to lock the deadbolt as the creaking of the porch was heard.

She held her breath. She had to stay right behind the door, or the creature would see her in the windows. She heard rustling and then a thump. The creaking stopped and it was silent again. Did it leave? Oh, how she hoped it had left. The thump? Did it leave something for her again?

First, she dared to peek out the window to the porch. She saw a glimpse of a huge towering and hairy figure disappear into the trees.

"Please don't be a dead animal." She whispered to herself as she stepped out to the porch. There was a lump of something wrapped in a brown paper bag. She picked it up and quickly went back into the house. It wasn't heavy but it smelled heavenly, not like a dead animal at all. When she opened it up, she realized the scent was dried berries, there was also some kind of dried beef and some wild nuts of some kind.

"Oh, sweet Sasquatch!" She hollered as she began to scarf down the meal. It wasn't really tasty, but good enough. Especially on an empty stomach.

Something odd was going on. This Bigfoot fellow— She assumed he was a fellow because well, monsters were always male, right? Okay, no. It just had a masculinity about it. But this Bigfoot had brought her heat when it snowed, and the lights went out and he must have heard her plea for food because now he brought her a meal. It was most definitely stalking her but so far it had not been unpleasant and yet, it was still the most frightening thing to ever happen to her.

Now she had been wined and dined, she wondered if she should try to meet the thing. Would it knock her over the head and drag her back to its cave? No, that was cavemen. What was the difference, she wondered, between a caveman and a Bigfoot? Wait. What had her life become? She quit her fancy marketing job in San Diego, she left her apartment and all her friends and family and now she lived with a Bigfoot suitor, calling at all hours. She couldn't tell if her life had really gone downhill or she was hallucinating.

At least now she had a relationship with a male whereas before, she did not. If it was a man. She was not sexist like that. It could be a female Bigfoot too; she just wasn't sure if the females were really masculine too or if it was just the men.

After contemplating the reality of the universe and filling her belly, Felicity felt like she could perhaps explore the area surrounding the cabin. Just not the woods because they were scary as hell. Just the parts that were clear, wide open spaces.

She booted up and zipped up her coat and ventured out. Being a Cali girl she couldn't remember a day that actually warranted the winter gear she had, but it looked like it wasn't going to be necessary here for long either, it was warming up and the sun actually popped out a few seconds at a time through broken clouds. The snow was quickly melting and there were even spots of visible dirt on the ground. Perhaps she wouldn't need Connor to get her out after all. She hoped he would come anyway, however, because she needed help with getting the electricity back on. She needed to charge her phone, take pictures of the place and get it listed on B&Bs.com. She thought she could stay in the master bedroom while the rest of the house was rented and that way, she could have free rent, make side income with the rentals and be around to maintain the house. She still wasn't sure how her Bigfoot stalker fit into all of this. Hopefully it didn't.

She meandered around the yard for a while but there wasn't much to see. Soon the clouds passed back over, and the dripping of the melting snow slowed. It was feeling much too cold for her again and she headed back inside, but as she passed her car she glanced at the back seat. There was the unmistakable side profile of a book peeking out from under her sweatshirt. *Mom.* She thought as she opened the car door and pulled out her well-worn copy of Pride and Prejudice. Her angel mother, distressed at the thought of her daughter uprooting and selling off her old life, had tucked the copy away without her knowledge, knowing how handy it could be under the right circumstances.

Cuddling up on the sofa and pulling an old but soft, yellow afghan up around herself, she passed the rest of the day reading until the sun went down and she hoped that Connor would be there soon because she couldn't read by the light of the stove and even though it was early it was already very dark.

She heard the crunch of wheels over gravel and the squeak of breaks. Connor had finally arrived!

Felicity went out to greet him.

"Boy am I glad you are here!" She said as she shook his hand and led him up the steps to the cabin.

"I thought you said it could wait until this evening. I could have come sooner."

"Yeah, I'm just really polite like that and don't like to put people out. The power has been out, and I'm stranded since I've dug my car in a bit." Felicity nodded toward her little gray civic, six inches deep in mud trenches courtesy of her revving her engine in an attempt to get out.

"Yeah, Ben always had a bit of trouble with the snow knocking out his power. I can pull your car out. If you park it over there," Ben nodded toward a little flat spot nearer the woods, "you should be able to get out easier next time. Ben put in a lot of work on that spot with gravel and what not, to prevent mud, so park there and then you can gun it next time it snows, and you should be fine."

"Oh, okay, good to know. I guess we could just move the car there now?"

"Sure." Connor said. Less than enthusiastic. It made Felicity feel bad that he had come out all this way. He probably wanted to be home with his wife or girlfriend right now and instead he was here with her.

"I'm really sorry you had to come out all this way. I really appreciate it."

"It's no trouble at all. I'm happy to help." He said, a bit more friendly, but Felicity wasn't convinced.

"I'm sure you'd rather be home hanging out with your family or girlfriend."

"Nope, I don't have a family and I had no plans tonight. I'm just sorry you had to sit here all day with no power, stranded like this."

So, maybe he wasn't upset after all. This guy was seriously hard to read.

Connor hooked up a strap to someplace underneath Felicity's bumper and then hooked it to the back of his truck. He gunned his engine and he fishtailed a little, but her car eventually bumped out of the trenches it was in.

"Hop in your car and see if you can get it over to the parking area." He said as he poked his head out his open truck window.

Felicity obeyed, it slid around a bit, but she was able to get it to the parking area just fine. She could feel how much more solid the ground was under her tires there.

She hopped out of her car and went to join Connor in the middle of the drive.

"Now, if you follow that line of the property, it's the same as the parking area and you shouldn't get stuck again. You need to stay out of this meadow area."

Felicity felt dumb. She hadn't realized that it was a meadow area. She just thought the whole thing was a cleared drive area. "Yeah, I will. Thanks again."

"Sure! Now, let's get your power back on."

Felicity thought she heard rustling in the woods to her right. Connor must have heard it too, because he looked over into the tree line.

"Let's get inside," He said as he pulled out a flashlight. "Don't worry, it's probably just a deer or a racoon."

"Yeah, probably." Felicity shuddered.

Once in the house Connor knew exactly where to go. He walked straight over to the circuit breaker and opened it up. He tried all of the switches, but the power remained off.

"Shoot, I was hoping it would be that simple."

"Yeah, me too." He looked at her in the dim light. "I already tried that."

"Oh, good girl. My wife wouldn't have thought of that."

"I thought you weren't married?"

"Ah, ex-wife."

"Ah."

"Well, I guess I need to go check around the back." Connor went to move but Felicity anticipated his movement wrong and bumped square into him.

"Sorry." He said and then chuckled. "I'll just- go this way." He maneuvered around her and headed toward the back-kitchen door. Felicity felt a spark for just a moment there and wondered if he felt it too. She took a deep breath and went to follow Connor but her eye caught movement in the bedroom window. She hurried after Connor, she wasn't sure if she would stop him or just hope that the creature went away. "Connor!" She called as she stumbled through the dark living room. He reached for the kitchen door and had his hand on the knob. He turned around expectantly, waiting for her to say something, then without warning the lights came back on.

"Oh, hey! I guess it kicked itself back on."

"Yeah. Great!" Felicity feigned pleasure at the returning power, but she knew that the creature had something to do with it. *The big jerk probably knocked it out in the first place.*

Connors phone dinged. He pulled it out of his pocket and spent a moment reading a message. "I better get going. Something's come up."

"Well, I can't thank you enough, really." He opened up the kitchen door and started to step out.

"I'll just go out this way."

"Oh, okay. Thanks again."

And with that Connor disappeared into the night. Felicity could hear his truck start and saw the headlights streak bright light across the living room window. Then it was quiet, except for the sound of the fridge compressor humming and the microwave occasionally beeping a message that it wanted the clock set.

Felicity felt a chill. It was starting to get cold in the cabin again. She still had a few logs and she felt if she started a fire now then went into town for some food, by the time she got back, the cabin would be toasty warm. Plus, she was stir crazy from being alone and bored all day and wanted to get out badly.

She plugged her phone in and watched a YouTube video on the best way to start a fire in a cast iron stove. It went much better this time as she used small slivers of wood to start the fire vs. trying to light an entire big log with just paper. The fire was roaring, and she shut the stove door and grabbed her coat. She was ready to rush to her car and get out of there. So far that creature had not bothered her. He had been helping her, but she had no intention of becoming a Bigfoot bride and was in no hurry to meet it. So, she ran to her car and locked the doors. She started the engine and began backing out of the parking area. There was still a lot of snow on the ground, even though some had melted. There was no way she could turn around so she thought she could just back out all the way down the driveway and turn around right before the road that led to the main road.

It went pretty well, she only slipped around once or twice, and she was on her way.

Felicity found the little store in town via Google maps. It was a decent size, nothing like the stores in the city, more like a drug store size than a grocery. They had mismatched carts, probably donated from other stores and she found it ironic that the store logo was of a lumbering Bigfoot and the sign said Squatty's. She spent a few minutes trying to find a cart that went straight as it was pushed. The only one that did also squeaked and bounced every time one of the wheels went around, but it pushed straight so it would have to do.

Felicity was starving so she bought up just about the whole store. Her cart was completely full by the time she had made a whole round of the place. She wasn't much for cooking, except for breakfast so she had a lot of convenience items in the cart. As the teenage checker with zits and curly hair checked her out, she saw Connor come through the sliding doors holding a woman by the hand. He made eye contact with Felicity. He awkwardly nodded and they disappeared down an aisle.

The checker kid nodded at Connor and chuckled to himself.

"What?" Felicity thought he was laughing at her.

"Nothing, it's just that guy's got a new chick every weekend."

"Oh, good to know." Felicity thought it strange, but she shrugged it off. It's not as though he owed her anything. His life was completely his own.

Felicity loaded the groceries into the back seat of her Civic, because her trunk was full of all the things from her old life that she deemed necessary or too sentimental to discard.

She was really looking forward to how cozy and warm the place would be when she got back and to being a little bit braver tonight and sleeping in the master bedroom.

As she pulled off onto the little dirt drive that led to the cabin, she began to have a bit of anxiety. She would have to unload all of these groceries, with multiple trips, into the cabin.

Maybe, if she did hear her large friend in the woods, she would ask for help with the groceries. She pulled up into the parking area and took a deep breath. She had left the front door unlocked, which was actually a good thing because she could sprint to the front door and not have to fiddle with unlocking it.

She opened the back door of her car and winced as the old door creaked loudly, announcing her arrival home. She grabbed as many bags as she could. She loaded two on the crook of each arm, she had three in each hand and one in her teeth. But there were still a few jugs of milk, juice and laundry soap, and a few bags of bread she would have to come back for. She trod through the mud and snow to the front door and somehow was able to turn the knob with her hands. As she opened the door, the cabin was wonderfully warm and inviting. She still didn't want to be too long with the front door open, so she ran to the kitchen and unburdened herself of all the bags she had.

Now, she ran back to the civic and before she could bend herself down to grab the rest of the groceries, she heard a rustling in the woods behind her on the other end of the driveway clearing. Her heart stopped and her breath caught in her throat. She turned around and out of pure stupidity and maybe a bit of nerves yelled, "Hey, why don't you stop gawking and come help me with these groceries." Even though she was scared, even though she knew something had been watching her, she really didn't believe that anything would come out of those trees.

With a rustle of a few branches and a crunch of earth beneath its massive feet the giant Bigfoot creature ducked out of the woods and began striding toward her. It limped slightly but it still came at alarming speed. It was dark and Felicity couldn't make out it's features clearly, just a large hairy silhouette of a being. Felicity screamed and jumped in her car, she prayed as she tried to get the keys back in the ignition. She looked back at the direction it was coming, and it had paused briefly, but then started to come at her again. She got the car going and slammed it into reverse without ever closing her rear driver-side door. She looked over her shoulder as she slammed on the gas, but it was hard to see where she was going, she thought she should turn the car around. She turned the wheel sharply and the car went into the meadow area. She couldn't see where it went, so she just slammed the gear into drive and hit the gas.

She heard a whirling and skidding, and the little car wouldn't move!

"NO!" She yelled as she looked in the rear-view mirror, the hulking figure was right behind her car, glowing red in the brake lights, its arm raised over its face to block the brightness. She tried putting the car into the low gear settings, when she heard its massive hands bang down on the trunk of her car and it growled as its massive arms pushed down on the trunk, again and again. The little car bounced, and Felicity slammed her foot on the gas again and the car fishtailed slightly. The creature pushed down on her car again, and finally her car gained some traction and she was off, down the road.

She screamed again to herself half in relief, half in fear. As she barreled down the little dirt road, she saw the puddle she had simply gone around before. This time, she was going to barrel through it because there was no time to correct. The front of her little car dropped in the deep puddle and hit the ground. From there she lost control of the car as it bounded out of the deep hole the puddle concealed, and off into the tree line. She tried to brake but her car hit some low shrubbery and perhaps a felled log and came to an abrupt stop. Felicity slammed the car in reverse and looked in the mirror, to her horror she saw the creature coming down the road toward her. It ran at an alarming speed!

She only had one option. She would have to get out of the car and run!

Felicity bounded out of the car and started running down the road. She hoped she would make it to the main road and maybe flag a car to rescue her. As she ran at full speed through the dark night, she could barely make out the road and the creature was right behind her. She could hear its heavy footsteps pounding on the ground behind her. She glanced back and she could see it gaining on her. She thought if she turned off into the forest, she could lose it by going through tight, densely packed trees that it couldn't navigate. So, she made a tight turn into the woods. But she had miscalculated because she was not adept at running on uneven ground, and she struggled to keep her speed. She could barely see where she was going, and she had to look down so she wouldn't trip. She was able to cut through some tight trees, but they scratched at her. She looked back a few times and she was right, even though she couldn't run as fast, she did gain some ground by ducking through the densely treed areas. She came upon an area where there were brambles and trees on both sides and a large log, there was nowhere to go but over the log.

Chapter Three

Felicity woke up with a massive headache. As she tried to open her eyes, the room spun. She had no idea how much time had passed but she realized she was in her cabin. She tried to move but she heard large, lumbering steps and creaking from the kitchen. She was laying in the bed in the master bedroom. She held her breath and listened. The Bigfoot was in her cabin! It had caught her, knocked her out and brought her back here! She looked over at the bedroom window and thought her only chance would be to escape out that way. The thundering footsteps got closer and she knew she had to act fast. She hopped out of the bed. She looked down at herself and she was not wearing boots or even socks and she also didn't have a coat on, she scanned the room quickly and there were no boots or coats to be found. She would have to run through the mud and snow barefoot. She went to open the window, but it wouldn't budge. She tried with all of her might, but it was locked. She tried to move the lock and it too would not give. The footsteps were just outside of the door now. She tried one last time to get the window to open and it cracked slightly, she tried to put her fingers in the little gap and pry it more, but it continued to be stubborn. Without looking she heard the footsteps enter the room and she froze. So many thoughts swirled through her mind. *Why had she stayed when she knew that creature was there? Why didn't she just go home? Why did she quit her job? She could have hired someone to just sell the cabin off.*

"Whoa! Hey!" She heard a deep soothing voice call out. She looked behind her to see a vision of a man. Tall, broad shouldered, handsome. His hair was cut short on the sides and long on top and he had a finely groomed, dark beard peppered with just the right amount of gray. He had piercing blue eyes and wore a red and black plaid shirt over tight jeans.

Felicity grasped at her chest and sighed heavily with relief.

"I- I thought-."

"I gave you quite the fright there, didn't I!" He said as he set a tray of food down on the side table and rushed over to help Felicity up.

"Yes, I didn't know who was coming down that hall."

"Well, don't worry, I'm perfectly harmless. I've patched up your head the best I could, but I think you have a concussion. No worries. I'll stay with you for the recommended twenty-four hours and make sure you don't fall asleep." Felicity glanced at herself in the mirror. She was a mess and had two black eyes forming as well as a deep gash on her forehead.

"Who are you?" She said as she gingerly touched her head injury.

"I'm Greg. Greg Thomas. I'm a friend of your uncle Ben. Or I was." Greg bowed his head momentarily. "I live a few cabins over." He said pointing towards the woods.

Felicity sighed a breath of relief. She was glad Greg found her before that creature did.

Greg led Felicity to the bed. "Here, you should rest. You've had a rough night." Felicity looked out the window, it still looked like night.

"Where's my phone?" She asked herself as she patted her pockets. "What time is it?"

"It's six am. Since I found you, you've been unconscious. I'm a former military medic so I hope you don't mind that I took it upon myself to clean you up and take care of you. I assure you that even though you were out so long that it didn't warrant an ER visit. Head injuries typically look worse than they are. But I will take you into the clinic first light, I promise."

"Thank you. I feel so lucky to have been found by you." Felicity didn't want to mention the Bigfoot chasing her the night before.

"I'm not sure why I scared you so badly, but I'm here to help. It's what your uncle would have wanted." He looked down solemnly again.

"Thank you. I've been jumpy since I arrived here."

"I can see that. A young woman, all alone in the woods for the first time?"

"Yeah, I'm from California. We don't have dense, dark forests like this there... Not down south anyway."

"Well, here." He put the tray on her lap, "eat."

"Thank you." She said as her eyes lingered on his for a little too long. He smiled. Wow. What a smile. He sat in the chair across the room and put his legs out.

A knot formed in her stomach. She grew cold with fear again as she glanced out the window. That creature would come back for her when he was gone, then what would she do? Could she ask this total stranger to stay with her until she was able to leave? "My car!" She cried out, remembering that she had crashed it.

"It's in the driveway, it's got a bent wheel and a few dings and scratches but it's still perfectly drivable."

"Oh, thank goodness. I need to get out of here." Felicity started to get up out of the bed after she moved the tray off her lap. As she stood, she felt a wave of dizziness wash over her. Greg jumped up and effortlessly lifted her off the ground and placed her back in the bed gently which greatly surprised Felicity as she wasn't a dainty thing.

"You aren't going anywhere until seven, when the clinic opens. They've got an MRI and they will check you out."

"Clinic?"

"Yeah, it's the best we got for a hospital around here."

"Okay, I'll wait." She glanced out the window again and Greg caught her looking.

"Hey, it's okay. You are safe with me. I promise."

Felicity nodded and picked up the glass of orange juice on the tray. She took a sip. Oh, it was good. She actually never ate last night. It turned her appetite back on.

While she ate, they talked about her uncle Ben.

"I didn't really know him. What was he like?"

"Oh, Ben was a rough guy. But I really liked him. He was about two feet shorter than me, so I wasn't scared of him. But he really kept to himself out here. He lived with a woman named Isabelle for a number of years, she fixed this place up really nicely as you can see. She left him a few years before he passed. He wasn't doing too well emotionally just before he went. I think he was more and more heartsick over Isabelle as the years went on."

"How sad. I can't imagine loving someone that much." Then Felicity looked at Greg's dazzling profile and realized that maybe she could.

"I've never found that kind of love myself, but I do spend a lot of time out here alone."

"Oh, why's that?"

"I used to be in the army. I saw a lot of things I'd care to forget. In the city, it's hard to forget. People treat each other badly and they don't appreciate what they've got. Out here alone, I just feel the peace I was searching for. I joined the army to bring peace to the world and I found out quickly that that's not what the army is for."

"What do you mean?"

"The army is the axe of whatever politicians are in power, to be wielded as they please, not for justice or peace, but mostly for money and power."

"Oh." Felicity found that sentiment to be incredibly deep. She had never thought about the army that way.

"But I learned a lot and made a lot of good friends who come and visit me from time to time but I don't get out to meeting a lot of ladies." He winked.

Felicity blushed. "I love it out here, it just——" She really wanted to tell him about her Bigfoot stalker but at the same time she really didn't want him to think she was crazy.

"You're scared. I can see that."

"Yeah. It's scary to be a woman alone in the world."

"You know what, you just need to be taught skills. A little confidence would help you feel more secure and safe. I think a woman is every bit as good as a man, it's just a matter of learning how to take care of yourself." He smiled. "I could teach you if you wanted to stay a while."

"Oh, thanks. That's really nice of you." It took every ounce of willpower for Felicity not to swoon. "I was planning on staying and running this place as a bed and breakfast."

"Oh, that's a great idea! Ben would love that you are doing that."

"Oh really? That's good. I wasn't sure what he would think."

"Oh, yeah, he told me before he passed that he had a niece he thought could use a place like this to call her own. I'm assuming he meant you."

"Yeah," Felicity chuckled. "I'm his only niece. I didn't realize he even really knew who I was."

"Oh yeah, he mentioned you a bit. I had a grandfather I didn't really know and after he died his wife told me stories about how I used to play with him when I was a tot. He always remembered me though I didn't really know him."

"That's right. I did see him regularly when I was very young."

"You must have been even cuter and left an impression on him." Felicity blushed as Greg stretched out and looked at his watch. "Time to go."

Felicity started to get out of bed, but he grunted and held out a hand for her to stop. He helped her put on her shoes and coat, then he swooped her out of bed and carried her out to the front of the cabin. She saw her little civic, beaten up and bumped but still drivable just like he said. Greg put her in an old, white, vintage ford pickup truck with blue stripes and buckled her in.

Felicity scanned the tree line but there was no Bigfoot or rustling to be heard.

"Thank you, for this. I assume my uncle was a decent enough human that he would appreciate your kindness to me."

"You're welcome. It's the least I can do."

"The least you could do for what?"

Greg shrugged, "So, where are you from?"

Felicity noticed the redirection, but her head hurt too much to make too much of it. "I'm from California."

"Yeah, you mentioned that, what part?"

"Oh, duh. San Diego. The best part."

"Hmm, I can see why you would think that. It's a pretty nice city. When are you going back?"

"As soon as possible."

"Not a fan of old growth forests and "yocals?'"

"Heh, no it's not that. I just— Don't think I belong here."

"I can see that. San Diego is a quiet city, but a city, none-the-less. I spent a few of my days off down there at the beach."

"Oh, what did you do?"

"Army Medic."

"Yes, I think you said that." Felicity pointed toward her bruised head as an explanation of her forgetfulness.

"Most of my time in the Army was spent serving in Iraq and South Korea, but when my tours were over, I chose to be based out of California. Couldn't afford San Diego on my E-nine salary though, so I only visited. What do you do in Cali?"

"I worked in marketing."

"Oh yeah? Doing what?"

"It's pretty complicated, and boring."

"Wait, you said worked, what do you do now?"

"I was hoping for a change of scenery, I sure got it."

"Are you going to start your own marketing business up here?"

"No."

Greg smiled and decided that maybe he would sit quietly for the rest of the ride. So, he turned up the radio and quietly sang along. Felicity didn't mind Greg asking her questions, it was just that she didn't want to give him the wrong answers. If she did end up leaving tomorrow and selling off the cabin, there was no point in striking up a conversation with him about her dreams of fixing up the cabin, but if she stayed, she didn't want him to think she was going to leave. He had added an element of uncertainty to her plans and this was after just a few moments of meeting him.

When they got to the clinic, it wasn't open yet, but Greg knocked and an office manager in scrubs let them in. Greg didn't need to explain she had bumped her head because of her bruised face, and they took her straight back to the MRI. After enduring the loud MRI clicking and buzzing, she was happy to sit in the quiet waiting room with Greg.

He leaned over and picked up a magazine. "You're going to be fine."

"I'm just so dizzy."

"It's temporary, you probably have a bit of swelling that is pushing on your optic nerve or your inner ear. Once the swelling goes down you will feel your old self again."

"Well, I guess we'll see what the doctor says."

"Right. No reason to worry until the doctor says otherwise."

She thought he was a wonder. He had taken something negative, her fear of the situation and transformed it into hope. It immediately endeared him to her more. Felicity had been looking for a person to be with for years, but all the guys she met at bars, speed dating and online were so shallow or just looking for a temporary hook up. One guy, Taylor, seemed like the perfect guy for many weeks, but as time went on, he showed his true colors more and more. He stopped holding doors open for her, he never introduced her, he was rude to waitstaff and he became more and more inattentive to her feelings. Finally, one night when Felicity thought he wanted to physically go farther than she was willing, he blew up in her face, calling her disparaging female terms and calling her an ice queen for not "putting out". Thankfully, the restaurant owner came over and escorted him out. That was over two years ago. Felicity had been more cautious of who she dated after that, but that meant slim pickings.

After an hour of waiting an old, gray haired doctor came out.

"Ah, Greg, I hardly recognized you." He shook Greg's hand vigorously. "All is well young lady, just a slight concussion, but I know Greg here can handle looking after you."

"Great!" Greg shook the doctor's hand and pulled Felicity to her feet. She shook the doctor's hand and allowed Greg to lead her back out to his truck. She didn't really know Greg. *Why had he taken ownership of helping her? He was just another one of those guys that like to show off what a knight in shining armor he could be... If you gave him what he wanted.* Greg helped her get back into the truck and this time, she buckled herself in.

"I'm really grateful for all of your help. It's incredibly kind of you."

"It's no trouble at all. I'm happy to help." Greg smiled and turned up the radio and sang along to Country Road. Felicity was starting to feel better and began to hum along herself. Which made Greg smile at her, which made her heart leap from her rib cage.

"I know you don't want to talk, but you don't mind if I do?"

Felicity felt bad, she did want to talk, badly. She had never wanted to tell someone everything so much before. "No, not at all."

"When I was in Korea, I was in a bar. I don't drink but I was hanging out with my buddies. It was a Korean bar but a lot of the Americans in the army went there. They served the best cheeseburgers you could find in Korea, almost like home, you know. So anyway, I was feeling kind of down that day because I had just been shot at earlier in the day."

"Oh my gosh, Greg."

"I was fine, but you tend to get shook up when someone shoots at you. We got a little too close to the border and there were some South Koreans crowding the border trying to reach the North Koreans who wanted to come across, neither side wanted their people to leave. They were estranged families and they were trying to reunite. Anyway, the North Koreans started firing into the crowd. A little boy got shot. I mean, can you imagine being the kind of guy who fires into a crowd with a bunch of kids?"

"No, that is horrible."

"Sorry, I didn't mean to get off track with that part of the story, it's depressing. Which is why I was at the bar. But this song came on the radio, and I had heard this song a million times back home. But for some reason that night, it really stuck with me. I started sobbing right there in the bar. I thought my buddies would come harass me about, you know, thinking I was weak or something. But they didn't, they just stood behind me and put their hands on my shoulders until I could compose myself. When I turned around, I saw that they all had tears in their eyes as well. The local Koreans had heard the story too, of what happened at the border and a lot of them had tears in their eyes too. That night I knew I was done with the army. I took an out, which left me with a dishonorable discharge. But I didn't care. I didn't want to be a part of the problem anymore."

Felicity sat silently as the song ended. Greg's eyes glistened slightly, as though he might shed a tear, but he didn't.

"You aren't like other men, are you?"

Greg laughed lightly, "I'm not sure if that is a compliment or not."

"Well, if I'm right, it is a compliment."

"Then no. I'm not like all those other jackasses!" They laughed and it made Felicity's head throb, but it was worth it.

When they arrived back at the cabin, he carried her back into the house. This time she laid her head against his strong chest and pulled his sweet woodsy scent into her nose.

He put her back in the bed. "Are you still dizzy?" He asked as he laid her down.

"A little, not nearly as much. Could you hand me those sweatpants over there?" He glanced over and saw a pair hanging over the side of her suitcase. He effortlessly reached and grabbed them.

"I'll be right outside the door if you need me. Call me right away if you feel like you might fall. A head injury this close to another will surely result in serious complications."

"Ok. Thanks." He left the room and shut the door. Felicity did feel dizzy, but she avoided having a hot stranger help her with her pants by changing them while lying on the bed.

"I'm good." She said as she threw her jeans across the room and missed her suitcase, then tucked her legs into the bedding. Greg came back in and picked up her pants then folded them neatly into her suitcase. Then he settled into the chair across the room.

"I'll be right here if you need me." He said then he closed his eyes and quickly fell asleep. Felicity was feeling quite tired herself. She felt safe with Greg there and nodded off to sleep with a smile on her lips.

Chapter Four

Felicity awoke to the sound of wood banging and crashing. At first, she froze thinking the Bigfoot had returned but then she realized she was hearing chopping. She looked at the chair and Greg was gone.

She sighed relief that her savior was still there, and he was probably chopping wood to get a fire going. It was getting dark and cold already. She felt much less dizzy and got herself up out of bed and shuffled her way out to the side door to greet Greg.

"Greg?" She called as she walked around the corner of the cabin. The snow had melted, and the birds were chirping the arrival of spring in the woods.

He didn't reply as he continued to chop wood. Felicity rounded the corner as Greg swung the axe down upon a full log of wood again.

"Hey!" She called. He turned to look at her and he smiled as his eyes met hers.

"Hey yourself." He said charismatically. "How are you feeling?" He set the axe down and began picking up an armful of wood.

"I feel much better, thanks. I guess you are free to go."

Arms piled high with wood he walked right past her, giving her a sly smile most of the way. "I'll just get this in the house for you. Then when I'm done with dinner, I'll go." He said as he pushed the kitchen door open with his foot.

Felicity tagged along after him. "Really, you don't have to do that."

Greg stacked the wood next to the stove in the living room. He looked around at all of Uncle Ben's mounted heads.

"I can stick around until you feel safer."

"I—" She couldn't argue with that. She had never been so frightened before and Greg had proven himself to be a trustworthy and helpful friend. "I'd appreciate that. I—" she paused, should she tell him about her Bigfoot stalker? "I seem to have a bit of a stalker since I've arrived."

"What? Do you know who it is?"
"Not who, it's more of a what."
He tilted his head in confusion, "what?"
"There's some sort of thing—"
"A cougar?"
"No."
"A bear?"
"Only if bears walk upright."
"Bears *can* walk upright, has it tried to get in?"
"No, it always walks upright and no, it hasn't tried to get in."
"Then what are you saying? Only a man always walks upright. Unless—" Greg froze in his swirling thoughts.
"Unless what?"
Greg jumped up and ran out to his truck through the front door.
"Do you know what it is?" Felicity trailed behind him and stayed on the front porch as she watched him pull a double barrel shotgun out of his truck, then he threw a rifle of some sort over his shoulder by a strap, grabbed a few boxes of ammo and headed back to the cabin. Felicity wasn't sure if she should be scared or impressed.
Greg trod back to the porch and looked around cautiously. "Let's get back inside. Quietly now."
"Do you know what it is?" She asked him again.
"I've never seen one. I've never known someone who's seen one. But I know people who know people who have seen one. You can't be too careful. Let's just say I've heard too many stories to take it lightly when someone tells me they've been stalked by one."
"By what? What do you think it is?"
Greg looked at her with a slightly obvious expression. "Sasquatch, Bigfoot, Skunk Ape, Abominable Snowman, Yeti, Yowie... It's got lots of names. That is what you are talking about, right?"
"Yes. It's just so ridiculous, but I swear I saw it multiple times."
"Well, like I said, I've heard too many stories to take it lightly. If you've seen something— I'm not leaving you here alone."
"They told me at the diner that it's never hurt anybody."
"That's true. No one that we know about. But I've heard one can take down a full-grown male bear. Can't be too careful. The only thing they are afraid of is a gun." He put his guns on the table behind the sofa. "What can I make you for dinner?"
Felicity blinked. "Whatever you can cook, I guess?"
"I've been on my own for a long time. Just tell me what you like, and I'll make it happen."

"I've got everything needed for a spaghetti dinner?"

"Great! I love Spaghetti!"

"Great." Felicity said, her mind still reeling from their Bigfoot conversation. She shook herself out of it. "I'll help."

"Are you sure?" He asked as he stepped close to her and inspected her face. His look was serious and composed. He pulled a small flashlight out of his pocket and shined it in her eyes. Then he gave her a piteous grimace. "You poor thing. That looks really painful." He gently turned her face side to side inspecting the gash on her forehead. "It should heal up nicely though." Felicity gazed into his perfect blue eyes. His pity transformed into a smile and he returned her gaze for a moment too long. Felicity blinked as he dropped his hands from her face and went back to pulling ingredients out of the fridge and placing them on the counter.

"Ben's got to have a pot around here somewhere."

"Oh, yes, I saw one." Felicity remembered one under the cabinets when she was scouring the place. "Here we are!" She said as she pulled the pot out and began filling it at the sink. She glanced outside and thought she saw movement in the tree-line, she froze in place and stared at the suspected movement.

"Felicity?"

"Huh?" She looked back at Greg who nodded toward the sink.

"Oh shoot!" She cried as she looked down and saw the pot had tipped and was overflowing over the countertop and down to the floor.

"You ok?" Greg said as he came over to the sink with a towel to help her clean up.

"Yeah, I thought I saw something out there."

Greg stood close to her and looked out the window with her.

"Right there?" He pointed to the same spot Felicity was looking at before.

"Yeah." She whispered back. They stood shoulder to elbow staring at the spot in the tree-line.

A large black bird flew out of the tree and right towards the window before swooping up to clear the roofline. Felicity screamed and Greg jumped.

"Oh!" He began to laugh, "That made me jump! Damn bird!"

Felicity began to laugh as well, as soon as she could breathe again. "I thought it threw something at the window!"

"What? Your Bigfoot?"

"Yeah. It's been watching me. I thought maybe it was jealous."

"Of me?" He laughed.

"Yeah." She sighed, embarrassed.

Greg grabbed the pot and put it on the stove. "How about a saucepan?" he said, shaking the jar of spaghetti sauce.

"Here." She pulled out another pan and handed it to him.

"Normally I wouldn't use a jar… But this is one of the better brands so I think I can make it work. I don't suppose you have any fresh garlic and basil?"

"Garlic, no basil."

"We can make that work."

"Where did you learn to cook? I've never dated a man who could cook, not even toast."

Greg made a funny face. "One, what kind of guys are you dating, and two, are we dating?" He flashed her a dashing grin.

"Well, you are making me dinner…"

He smiled even bigger and looked down and away from her, "I've lived alone many years out here in the middle of nowhere, if I was craving something, I had to learn how to make it. Do you cook?"

"Yeah, I've lived alone for a long time too. It's not very fun to cook for one though."

"That's true. I used to cook for my girlfriend, but I've been on my own for a few years now."

"I have a hard time believing that *you* can't find a girlfriend."

He shrugged. "I wasn't much interested in one after the hell the last one put me through."

"Oh, I'm sorry." Felicity said as she pulled the parmesan wedge from the fridge and shuffled through a drawer for a cheese-grater. "I've not had luck in that department either."

"*Kristin*. She wasn't impressed with my dishonorable discharge."

"Did you explain to her why you had to do it?"

"Yeah, but she was an army brat. Her family lived and breathed army. There's no excuse for anything less than being honorably discharged and with a chest full of medals and shrapnel. Retire, or die."

"You still hold a candle for her?"

"Oh no!" He said as he stirred the pasta sauce a few turns and then started to peel the garlic. "We have completely different value systems and it doesn't matter how much you love someone if you don't have the same values it's nearly impossible to make it work. Over time, the candle goes out as you come to terms with that."

"The last relationship I had that was even worth pining over was a boy from high school. *David.* Funny enough, we actually never really dated, but we should have. He's happily married now, so it doesn't matter. But I do tend to beat myself up over letting him slip away from time to time."

"Now you are going to have to explain to me how *you* are still single."

"HA!" She said more than laughed. "I'd like to think it's not me, but— It must be me. Either that or I have the worst gauge of character on the planet."

"Maybe your gauge is too good, and you just can't find someone good enough for you."

"Yeah! Let's go with that." Felicity shied away from Greg. He was too good to be true.

They sat down with their plates full of steaming spaghetti and salad. After sleeping most of the day she was famished and barely spoke. Greg was good at making small talk and keeping the conversation light for the rest of the meal.

"Well, you get to resting on the couch and I'll clean up." he said as Felicity pushed her plate away.

"No, I can help. I'm feeling much better, really." She got up and took the plates and silverware while Greg gathered the pot of spaghetti and the salad bowl. "I don't know what you did but I swear that was better sauce than what should come out of the jar."

"I didn't do anything. It's the company that makes the dinner better."

Felicity blushed slightly and began scrubbing the plates with soap and a cloth.

"I've always loved this place." He said as she put the leftovers in a bag. "I've always dreamed of having a place like this."

"What's your place like then?"

"Oh, it's— Rustic."

"Running water?"

"Not really."

"Oh, wow."

"Every day is like an adventure with no power, water or heat. My cabin is a self-built four-hundred square foot off grid paradise. Maybe not for the ladies, but it's plenty of space for me."

"What do you do with yourself?"

"It takes quite a bit of time to cook and clean each day, without modern conveniences. I rescue ladies in distress. I hike a lot. I've been cataloguing the wildlife in this area. I discovered a beetle that has previously never been catalogued."

"Interesting. I'm not into beetles but I appreciate the academic curiosity."

"I wasn't into beetles either, until I came out here for the peace and tranquility. While I was out getting lost in nature, I discovered how interesting the life cycle of a beetle is. From larva to pupa to beetle. It's a fantastic journey of transformation. Much like my own."

"You see yourself as a beetle? I see." Felicity dried the plates and put them back into the cupboard. "I used to be a marketer for an insurance company. Like, a really good one. I was busy all the time. I was so busy that I didn't realize how empty my life was. So, when Uncle Ben left me this place, I thought it would be a good chance to stretch my legs a little. To just be, instead of always do."

"I know exactly what you mean." Greg winked and took his apron off that he was still wearing from making dinner. He carefully hung it in the pantry cupboard on a hook. "Well, I had a lovely evening. I'm going to stoke the fire a bit and then I'll be off to bed."

Felicity was about to ask him what bunk he wanted to sleep in when he held up his hands. "I'll sleep in my truck. I want you to feel safe but not put out."

"No. Greg, please, there is a bunk room you can take." Then Felicity imagined his tall frame and his feet hanging off the end of the beds. Still it was better than sleeping in a truck. "You can take the master bedroom bed and I'll sleep in the bunk room."

"Absolutely not! This is your cabin, I will be happy sleeping on the floor, you don't need to give up your bed for me."

"I've barely slept in it since that thing has been poking around here. I've been sleeping on the couch."

"Don't worry. Once it gets wind that I'm staying here it will leave for good."
"You think?"

"I know. I haven't seen it once. And I've been all over these woods. That can only mean one thing. It's avoiding me."

"I can see why."

Greg tilted his head in question.

"Oh, I meant because you are very- manly. Please take one of the queen beds, or the loft."

"Ah, well thank you for the compliment, I think. I guess I'll take the first guest room. Tomorrow, I'm going to teach you how to chop wood. You've got to have lots of skills to live alone in the Pacific Northwest! I'll see you in the morning!" He chimed as he walked down the hall and into the guest bathroom.

"Goodnight." Felicity sighed and then she shuffled herself off to bed. She slept soundly knowing that Greg was just down the hall.

The next day Felicity awoke to the sound of chopping wood again. She was glad that Greg was still there. It had been two days and she already couldn't imagine life without him. There were just some people that you didn't need to contemplate whether or not they fit into your life. You just knew. Today she would make *him* breakfast. She cracked open the fridge and pulled out everything she could think of for the best gourmet breakfast. She piled fruit high on a plate and cooked hash browns and sausage, then she pulled out the big guns and popped open a can of biscuits and a jar of country gravy.

"Smells great!" Greg said as he came back in, smelling of the outdoors. He came over by Felicity standing over the oven stirring sausage crumbles into the gravy. He put his arm around her and squeezed her shoulders in a friendly way. "You're not a bad cook yourself, are you?"

"I wouldn't call this cooking, more like reheating."

"Hey, I've been living off of jerky and wild berries for a season, I'll eat anything and call it gourmet!"

Felicity laughed and Greg got some dishes out of the cupboards.

"Juice?" He asked as he opened the fridge.

"Yes, apple please."

"As you wish." He winked and filled a glass and set it on the table then he poured himself some orange juice.

"I'd love to see your place."

"I'd love to show you." He said as he put the biscuits in a bowl and set it on the table.

"Great. Then you can teach me to chop firewood."

"Don't think I forgot. I've got a few other lessons lined up for you as well."

"Oh yeah? Like what?" Felicity brought the gravy pot over to the table and set it on a hot pad.

"Well, for starters, how to get the power back on when it snows."

"Oh, Ben told you about that huh?"

"Oh, yes. It happened every single time. We used to take turns turning it back on at poker night."

"What else can you teach me?" Felicity felt compelled for him to compile a list so she knew how long he would be around. Or at least how many excuses she had to see him.

"Everything you need to know to survive out here. What if you got lost on a hike?"

"I won't be hiking alone as long as that thing is out there."

"Fair point, but let's suppose it is gone and you are out hiking and get lost? I can teach you how to find your way back, or quite simply how to mark your trail, so you don't get lost in the first place. Or how about how to find food, build a fire, filter water."

"Sounds like you know everything."

"I know a lot about survival, that is true. What I don't know a lot about is you." He looked up from pouring gravy on his biscuits with a mischievous smile.

"Ah, well there's not much to me really. Remember? I've spent my adulthood working day and night to build someone else's wealth. He was out living life and I was providing the means for him to do so."

"I see. That's how I felt about the Army. Don't get me wrong, I'm proud of my service, but it wasn't as much of serving the American people as it was serving the politicians."

"I guess we are both out here looking for the same thing."

"Ourselves."

Felicity nodded and smiled, then dug into her breakfast.

Greg tried to teach Felicity how to chop wood, but her hands were a bit too soft and her arms too weak to do much. She was able to split a few logs, but she quickly fatigued and then had to nurse a large blister on her hand. Greg, as a military medic quickly cleaned and fashioned a comfortable bandage for her. "Don't give up. You will toughen up. I had a few blisters myself the first year I spent out here."

"You? You seem like the perfect specimen of a lumberjack." She laughed.

"Ha! I'm tough but you have to build up tolerances to different tasks. You can do it. Don't give up."

"I don't intend to." She said as she stared intently into his blue eyes. He held her bandaged hand gently in his and returned a longing look.

"I hope you are staying for a long while."

"I'm not planning on ever leaving."

"What about your job? You don't think you'll ever go back?"

"Never." She said as she studied his masculine jawline covered in a well-groomed beard.

"Good. I like that you are here." He said as his body seemed to involuntarily move toward hers as if she had a gravitational pull. She involuntarily looked at his full lips.

"I'm going to get this place updated and rented out, it's going to take months." She smiled as her heart quickened.

"That's an excellent idea." He said, so close now that their noses would touch if only, he hadn't turned his head ever so slightly to the side.

Time stood still now as Felicity expectantly waited for him to kiss her. She could feel the static electricity between them. He lifted his hand and put it on the nape of her neck.

They both jumped as they heard a crash outside of the front door. Faster than she could imagine a man his size moving, he was to the front door with his shotgun. Her heart was pounding even harder now with the jolt of adrenaline that coursed through her, fraying her nerves.

He threw open the front door just in time to see a fat, round racoon rear running into the trees.

"Oh, it's just a little racoon momma. I thought it was your Bigfoot boyfriend."

"My what?" Felicity laughed.

"Your Bigfoot stalker. I thought maybe he was watching us and was feeling jealous." He winked.

Felicity shuddered then sighed. "Do you still believe me? That I've seen a Bigfoot?"

"Of course, I do." He locked the front door and quickly joined her back on the sofa. He took her hands in his again.

"Ouch." She said quietly. He lifted her injured hand to his mouth and kissed it gently.

"Sorry." He said softly. "You looked really scared."

"I don't think I've ever been so scared since the moment I got here."

"You are safe with me, I promise. It was just a racoon family playing on the roof. You haven't seen your boyfriend since I've been around, right?"

"No, I guess not." Felicity smiled relief at him. Maybe he was right, the Bigfoot avoided Greg and so as long as he was around, she would be free of it. That didn't bother her one bit.

Greg looked out the window then back at Felicity. "Come on, it's getting late and I should show you my place before it gets dark. There's no electricity you know."

Chapter Five

Greg's old truck rumbled down the road as his country music blasted.

"Where did you grow up, Greg?" Felicity shouted over the music. Greg smiled at her and turned the radio down.

"Here and there. Mostly in Arizona, the Tucson area. Then I moved to Colorado just before I joined the military. From there it was Texas, Utah, California— Even Iraq was home for a while."

"This is really the first time that I've ever left California. I've been to Nevada a few times and Arizona, but I've always lived in the same place."

Greg pulled off the road and down a hidden lane, much like the one to her cabin.

"Hang on, it's quite a long and winding road from here." He chuckled.

He wasn't kidding, the road was full of potholes and wash outs, there were trees right in the middle of it that had to nearly be circumnavigated. They even drove over a perilous looking, handmade wooden bridge that was barely wide enough for his truck.

"Wow, are you trying to not be found?"

"Kind of." He laughed.

Finally, they arrived at a little clearing with a tiny cabin perched on the edge. It was cute and very rustic, compiled of various used and mismatched materials. The roof was made from several different colors of shingles and the logs looked as though they had been hand hewn.

"I built this myself." He said proudly.

"It's cute." Felicity smiled as she let herself out of the truck.

"I lived in an old army tent for a whole year while I did it."

"Wow, you are handy!"

"I only spent three-thousand on the whole thing. Most everything was either salvaged, harvested or donated."

"Can I see inside?"

"You bet, come on in. I'll show you how the gravity fed water system works." Greg took her up the much smaller porch than her own cabin and opened the door. It was unlocked. Inside was a small combination living room/ kitchen and a single door to the left, Felicity could see beyond that door was a bed. The ceiling was vaulted and there was a loft above the bedroom. The kitchen was free of appliances except for a small, black cast iron stove that served as a cooktop as well and a stainless-steel sink sunk into an old laminate countertop.

"So, I told you I don't have running water, and technically, I don't. There's no pump, there's no water heater, but—" he turned on the faucet and water came out. "I have a tank on the roof that creates enough gravity pressure to have running water."

"Do you have a shower too?"

"Uh, well, come and see. You might not call it a shower." He led her through his little bedroom with a tidy bed with rustic linens on it and he opened a door that seemed to lead outside the cabin. It was a small, lean-to like attached bathroom. There was a funny looking toilet and a galvanized steel stock tank that was roughly the shape of a tub but much smaller. Hanging from the ceiling was a shower curtain and a shower head. "I have another tank on the roof that feeds this shower, it is insulated, and I can fill it with hot water. So, I get a shower but it's a bit of work, I usually just fill up the basin and take a bath. She couldn't see how he could fit in that basin for a bath, but she was still impressed. Not only was his little cabin functional, it was also all built with style and thought for aesthetic appeal.

"Everything is really great. I could live here."

"Really?"

"Yeah," She said as she touched his plaid towel hanging from what used to be part of a lamp turned towel holder on the wall. "I love what you've done with it. It's really quaint and rustic."

"Thanks. Come on, I'll show you my beetle collection, if that's okay?"

"Yeah, please, show me!" Felicity wasn't particularly interested in beetles, but she was interested in what was so interesting to him about them.

He took her into the living room and pulled out a box. Inside the box were dozens of small shadow boxes and in each of those was dozens of beetle specimens pinned to the backing.

He had carefully labeled each specimen by Latin name, beautifully handwritten.

"Wow, these are works of art!" Felicity said. As she shuffled through the various shadow boxes. "Wow, look at this one, it's like an oil slick on water."

"I wanted to hang them up, but there's not a lot of wall space in here."

My Bigfoot Boyfriend

"Are they special to you? Because I think you could sell them as wall art."

"Really? Thanks, that's part of why I do it, I just think they look cool."

"Is there a gift shop or some sort of farmers market? I mean it Greg; I think you could sell these as art. I'd love some for my cabin. I think most guests would think these were really cool."

"Well, here." Greg handed her the last few she was looking at. "Take these."

"I'll pay you for them." She smiled.

"No, you won't."

"Yes, I will, what kind of person do you think I am?" Felicity asked, confused at his accusation.

"No, you won't because I won't let you. They are a gift."

"Oh." She felt stupid for thinking he was being rude. "Thank you."

"You're welcome." He said as he put his arms around her shoulders and pulled her in close. Her head naturally gravitated toward him and she snuggled into him. She was falling so hard for Greg, but life had taught her that no one is perfect and most of the men she had met were charming and handsome at first until they let their guard down. So, she sighed, but let herself enjoy the sweet tenderness of the cuddle while it lasted.

"It's getting dark. I can barely see anymore." Felicity said.

"Yeah, I need to stop off at the market to pick up some things. Is that okay with you?"

"Of course."

After Greg picked up a propane tank, some matches and a few other odds and ends, they walked out of the little store together. Once again, Felicity was confronted by Connor at apparently the only hangout in town. It wasn't hard to believe since the town boasted a grocery, drug store, gas station and the diner, that was it.

"Hey Felicity, hey Greg, I see you've met Ben's niece."

"Hey Connor, how are you? Yeah, I've been helping her out."

"You still seeing Bigfoot?" Connor laughed, but it seemed like he was laughing at her more than with her.

"No. Not since Greg's been hanging around."

"Oh," Connor looked uncomfortable. "You've been staying there?"

"Well, she had a bit of an accident as you can probably see, and I've been helping out."

"Oh, yeah, that looks— pretty bad." Connor said eyeing her bandaged forehead and blackened eyes. Felicity was struck with the fact that he didn't mention her injuries first thing like a normal, caring person would.

Greg shifted the propane tank, "Well, I'm going to get this in the truck, don't let me stop you from catching up," he said as he left Felicity standing there with Connor in front of the grocery.

"Are you okay? You need anything?"

"I'm in good hands, thanks." Felicity said, sensing that Connor was worried about her.

"Uh, yeah. I mean Greg's a super nice guy, even my girlfriend would take him in a heartbeat." Connor said with a bit of a sneer.

"I thought you didn't have a girlfriend."

"Uh— Yeah, um, the other day when we talked, I didn't and now I do. So, sorry about that, were you, uh, hoping to hook up or—" He almost seemed cocky for a moment.

"I really appreciate your help and your kindness upon me arriving in town, but I— No." Felicity pursed her lips in a tight smile and then nodded. "Well, I'll see you around," and she headed for Greg's truck.

"Yeah, sure." Connor said and turned to leave the wrong way, spun and then went the other direction.

Greg was already in the truck and Felicity jumped in. "He's a bit of an odd one."

"Yeah, nice guy though."

"Yeah. Just seemed like he wanted to take me out, then he turns up twice with a different girlfriend."

"Yeah, that's Connor. He's married too. Well, they are split but they still haven't finished the divorce."

"Oh, wow. Trying not to judge, but judging a little— Gotta admit."

Greg laughed lightly. "He's just doing his best."

"Aren't we all." Felicity said, more of a statement than a question.

Chapter Six

Felicity awoke to Greg lightly knocking on her door.

"Good morning." He said in a singsong voice.

"Hey." She squeaked, trying to sound awake.

"Here you go sunshine." Greg laughed as he handed her a cup of tea.

"Oh, thank you." She said with more control to her voice, sitting up in bed. Greg laughed as he smoothed down some of her hair. Felicity frowned in apology for her disheveled appearance.

"You look great." Greg said with a smile and he smoothed her hair again.

"To what do I owe this wakeup call?"

"It's the most beautiful sunrise I have ever seen, and I want you to see it too."

"Oh, I didn't know you had sunrises here, because of the trees."

"Well, come and see for yourself." He said holding up her robe.

She slipped her arms in one at a time, switching the tea from one hand to the other. Greg took her to the stairs, and they climbed them to the loft. The window was open, and he took her tea from her and placed it on the bedside table. "After you."

"What?"

"The roof."

"We are going out on the roof?" She said as she began to climb out the window. "Oh, wow." She gasped as Greg followed. She could see the mountains in the distance, that she couldn't see from the ground. They were majestically splendid in grays and blues, tipped with white that was reflecting the pinks and oranges from the rising sun. The juxtaposition of the deep blues and grays to the bright pinks and oranges nearly took her breath away.

"See, worth it." Greg sighed.

"I had no idea I was missing this every morning."

"Not every morning, just the clear one's."

Greg pulled her in under his arm as she shivered slightly. Again, her head tilted into his gravitational pull and they sat together in silence until the sun shone too brightly to look at anymore.

Over breakfast Felicity sighed. "I've got to get this place fixed up... I can't put it off any longer. I hate the aesthetic of dead animals. Do you think Uncle Ben would roll in his grave if I got rid of them?"

"I don't think it matters anymore. You can't live your life worried about what a dead uncle you barely knew would think."

"Hmm, good point. Will you help me? Can I put them in the back of your truck? Maybe I can take them into town and give them away."

"That's not a bad idea. These are worth a lot of money."

"They are? Why would people pay so much for a dead animal?"

Greg pointed to the biggest one. "That's a ten-point whitetail. There's a few hobby hunters that would pay good money for that."

"Oh, great! Well maybe I could sell them outside the market?"

"Put 'em on Facebook, then they will come to you."

"You are really smart. I like you." Felicity smiled. He returned a smile and raised her a wink. They had yet to kiss after that night that the racoon had interrupted their moment. She was beginning to think that there was something wrong with her. There were cuddles and shoulder squeezes, but that was it.

"Anyway, where is the nearest hardware store? I think I'm going to try to paint the rooms, and the kitchen."

"Just don't paint the logs." He said before gulping down some coffee.

"Well, I thought I could glaze them in white in the bedrooms. I saw this in a magazine, hey look," She said as she got up and ran to the living room and grabbed a magazine called CABINS and turned to a dog-eared page, "See? It looks really great and it doesn't hide the woodgrain too much but lightens up the place. This place could really use some lightening up."

"You're right! That looks great."

"I really like your style; I'd really love it if you would give me some pointers."

"Pointers? I'll do more than that, I'll be here by your side every step of the way, my friend."

"Friend?" Felicity blurted out the question before she could process it. Then she spoke again before he could say anything else. "That's amazing, thank you so much. I'm just going to go get ready and find the nearest hardware store. Or the biggest rather, I'm sure Bobby's hardware isn't going to have this glaze, you know?" And she rushed off to her room and locked the door behind her.

She felt really stupid. He wanted to just be friends and she had basically let it slip that she already thought they were more than that. She hoped that Greg was like most men and wouldn't notice it, but she knew he wasn't. He noticed. She pulled her hair up into a cute messy bun and threw on her jeans and t-shirt then pulled on a zip up hoodie. It was finally getting warm and she would probably have to put the hoodie around her waist by noon.

She spent a few minutes fixing her face and looking for the nearest Big Box hardware store. There was one about an hour away. That could be a long awkward drive after her little slip in the kitchen.

She opened her bedroom door and to her surprise, Greg was standing right outside.

"Oh!" She jumped slightly, "You ready to go?"

"No."

"Do you need to run home?"

"I know that we haven't known each other long. And I didn't want things to move too fast. I just feel really safe, happy, and content when I'm with you. I feel like we fit together in a way that is better than romance, it's friendship. It's—"

"Greg, it's fine. You don't have to explain. We do barely know each other, even though it feels like we've known each other forever, we can be friends if that's what you want. I will always be your friend first."

"See, that's what I mean. I know you will always be there for me, as a friend. I—
"

Felicity wanted to be done with this awkward conversation that wasn't going the way she wanted so she tried to slip past Greg to leave. "Greg, really, you don't have to let me down easy. I'll be fine, it's not as if we—."

He grabbed her arm and pulled her into him and kissed her. It didn't feel like any kiss she had ever experienced. Kissing was nice in general, but this kiss could be felt more with emotions than touch. This kiss was the most real thing she thought she had ever experienced. He put his hands around her waist and picked her up. She put her arms around his neck.

"That was nice. So— more than friends?"

"Way more." He whispered and pulled in her for another kiss. Her stomach leapt as she let her body melt into his. His hands pulled her in as close as possible, and she never wanted the moment to end. But it had to end, here in the hallway, so she came up for air. They held each other close for a few moments, breathing each other in. Felicity spoke first.

"Come on! We've got to get this place cleaned up fast! It's spring, and that means I will have bookings come summer, but not if we don't get this done!"

"As you wish!" He picked her up and threw her over his shoulder. Felicity laughed and grunted.

"Ah! Put me down!" She kicked her legs a little in protest and he pulled her down but then carried her in his arms like a knight in shining armor and put her in his truck. He reached over to buckle her in and stole another kiss.

"So, what's your plan?" Greg asked as his handsome brow raised at her.

"Well, number one is lunch. There's got to be somewhere cozy and special I could take you while we're in the big city."

"Wow, you are going to wine and dine me before you put me to work? I like it."

"Yes. Then after a nice lunch, the hardware store."

"Do you know what you are looking for?"

"Do I— Do I know what I am looking for? It's like you barely know me."

Greg shrugged good humoredly as Felicity pulled out a three-page list of items.

"Paint, white, two gallons. Box of wood screws, five by five rug, three-foot shelf, rustic. Pan organizer. Toilet paper, I think they carry that there. Glaze, three gallons, tinted in mountain wisp."

Greg interrupted her, "I don't know why I ever doubted that you had this... What about the shingles?"

Felicity's face fell. "The shingles! I did forget the shingles. Wow, Greg. I don't know what I would do without you!"

"You'd drive back and forth from the hardware store at least twice, that's what."

"Oh, that's the truth! What else do you think I forgot?"

"I don't know, keep reading."

"Mop, bathroom faucet, linen cupboard, downspout extender, dryer vent tube stuff—"

"What about the curtain in the loft? I think you need a new bracket for the rod."

"Oh, I didn't even notice. You remember what kind?"

"Yeah, I'll show you at the store."

They continued down the list and Greg filled in any gaps in Felicity's knowledge of repairs needed.

As they arrived at the big box hardware store, Felicity couldn't believe their luck. Connor was coming out the door just as they were going in.

"Hey, you two seem to be hitting it off pretty well?" Connor said awkwardly as he sized up Greg again.

"Yeah, she's got a lot of work to be done and I've got a lot of time."

"Yeah, I'm sure that's a big motivator for you."

Felicity could read between the lines; she couldn't deny that she had thought the same thing at first. That Greg was only helping out because he wanted something from her. After two weeks of paling around and never even landing a move until this morning, she was thinking that either he was really bad at the game, or he really did just want to be around her.

"Well, we've got to stop running into each other like this Connor. Maybe you should bring your girlfriend over for dinner some night? Preferably after I am done fixing the place up."
"Yeah?" Connor asked, as if she couldn't possibly mean it. "Okay, how about we come and help too? Tomorrow night?"

"Well, I wouldn't turn down good company and good help! I look forward to meeting- what was her name?"
"Ruby." Connor smiled.
"You are back with Ruby?" Greg asked. "That's great!"
Connor looked like he had been gut punched for a moment. "Uh, nope, my girlfriend is Gina, uh Tina. I— Mis-heard the question."
"Okay. We'll see you and Tina tomorrow night." Felicity smiled and started walking past Connor, bothered again by his complicated love life.
"See you Connor." Greg waved. As they each grabbed a large, oversized, orange cart Felicity sighed. "I know what you are thinking. He was one of the first people to help you when you came into town. He's a nice guy."
"He has no idea who he is married to or dating."
"No, but he's just going through a hard time."
"You're really sweet. Too sweet for this world maybe."
"It's not that, it's that I've seen things that are so— much worse that I know that Connor is a good guy. Even if his romantic life is a bit of a mess."
"I never thought about people like that before."
"Most people are really good, even when they are kind of a mess." Greg said followed by a heavy sigh.
"I feel like every time we see him, he is jealous. He actually had his chance and he literally walked out for another chick that night."
"What do you mean Connor had a chance?" Greg stopped in the middle of the lightbulb aisle.
"Yeah, before I met you. He was over and he had just pulled my car out of the snow. He bumped into me in the hall and it seemed like, you know."
"No, I don't know. What?"
"Like there was a little spark."
"Why are you telling me you had a spark with Connor."

"I'm just being honest. I think that's why he's always so awkward around you. But don't worry about it. You are cute when you are jealous!" Felicity blushed and started down the aisle again.

"I'm not jealous." Greg let go of his cart and grabbed Felicity's shoulder. He spun her into his arms, dipped her and planted a delicious kiss on her lips, "Why would I be jealous of sparks when we have lightning?"

An older gentleman down the aisle covered in dry paint laughed lightly.

"Greg!" Felicity laughed, seeing two more people eyeing his dramatic display of public affection. "You're so cute and embarrassing. But I like it."

Greg raised an eyebrow and smiled.

They flitted around the store like two lovesick teens and laughed and joked as they checked off Felicity's list.

Chapter Seven

"The place looks great, Ellie!"

"Thanks Mom, and there's someone I want you to meet! This is Greg."

Greg craned his neck over to be in view of the webcam. "Hi! It's nice to meet you!"

"Wow. He's really hot, Ellie."

"Mom!"

"Thanks! You're not so bad yourself."

"Oh my gosh you two! Stop it! Okay, I've got to go. I have some guests arriving at noon and it's nearly ten. Love you, Mom! Bye!"

"Bye Ellie, take care of each other, it's nice to meet you Greg!"

"Bye Mom!" Greg said and waved.

Felicity shut her laptop and leaned over to kiss Greg. "I think your mom likes me."

"No, she's just polite. She really didn't like you."

"Wow, how does she treat people she does like?"

"Ha ha, in all seriousness, she really does treat everyone the same. You would never know if she did like you or not. She's a *very* kind person."

"Well, I love her already."

"And I love you." Felicity bit her bottom lip. Neither of them had said *I love you*, yet. Greg tilted his head like a puppy and gave her a half smile. He reached over and put his hand gently around the nape of her neck and kissed her.

"I love you too." He finally said, his forehead pressed against hers. "I've never felt this way about anyone, ever."

"Me neither," she admitted as she stroked his beard lovingly. "Come on. I've got a lot to finish before the guests get here."

"Well, count me in little lady!" He said in an old-timey, western accent as he pushed off the couch and took her hand. He gave her a little dance spin, dipped her and finished it off with one more kiss. She always felt one hundred percent secure in Greg's arms.

They had a lot of cleaning to get through, Felicity had read that a B&B needed to be perfectly clean. Not a speck of dust would do. Plus, they had just barely finished redecorating the rooms and there were a few odds-and-ends tools lying around.

She decided she wanted to modernize and lighten up the interior of the cabin. She was going for more grays and whites and less browns. They painted the kitchen cabinets a dark teal blue. She knew it was risky, but it looked good in the end. It went great with the dark stained butcher block counters and the dark stained wood floors. She replaced the vintage kitchen table with something bigger and white to lighten up the room. It was a double pedestal table with a nice, light gray top and white legs. The chairs were all white too, with heavy wicker seats. She painted Uncle Ben's old pine shelves with the white glaze and put some woodsy knick knacks on them with a sign that said "Call of the Wild" in a handwritten font and the silhouette of a wolf on it.

In the living room she kept the yellow couch and the old rug and just updated the wall hangings. She decided to keep Uncle Ben's ten-point buck but got rid of the other half a dozen mounted heads he had. She replaced the heads with local artist paintings of the mountains and wildlife. She also updated the TV to a flat screen and had a satellite installed.

She decided the bathroom needed some brightening, so she glazed the outside walls made of logs with the white glaze and painted the interior walls white. She liked the many rustic things Uncle Ben had incorporated over the years but hated the nineteen-seventies elements everywhere, like the sparkly yellow laminate counter in the bathroom, so that had to go. The pine-branch towel bars and the rustic pine log shelves all stayed.

In the bunk room she updated all the linens and pillows and put red plaid flannel duvets on all the beds. It reminded her of Greg since he wore a red plaid flannel nearly every day, except the days he wore a white and black one or a blue and red one.

In the third and fourth bedroom she painted the walls with the white glaze, put a black metal queen size bed in one and left the brass one in the other and hung a picture Greg found for her. It was a painting of a Pacific Northwest, old growth forest with a hidden Bigfoot hiding in the trees. The picture was beautiful and reminded them of how they came together, plus it made her chuckle every time she walked by it.

"Alright, I think we have everything ready!" Felicity jumped with excitement. "I can't believe I got a booking with barely any pictures. Oh! We should take pictures before they get here so I can update the website!"

"I'll help, you get the bedrooms and bath and I'll get the rest."

The six guests arrived and settled in. It was a family from Tacoma. They raved about how great the place looked and then quickly left their belongings and headed out for outdoor fun. Felicity fussed about the first breakfast she needed to cook for strangers and read some books, updated her website and then it got dark. Greg had gone home for the night after cuddling with her while she read. He started a fire for her before leaving.

It had been since Greg arrived that Felicity had seen any sign of her Bigfoot boyfriend. She had almost forgotten about it and was starting to think that it was all her hyped-up imagination with the stress of moving and leaving her old life behind. As she sat in the living room waiting for her guests to come back, she thought she might make them some hot cocoa to enjoy. It was getting late and surely, they would be back any minute now. Felicity was busy in the kitchen laying out mugs, spoons and heating milk over the stove when she heard and felt a large disturbance of trees in the tree line. She could see a hulking creature bent over and pushing through the forest.

"He's back!" Felicity cried out to herself, her veins running cold with fear. She grabbed her phone and called Greg. "He's back!"

"I'll be right over. Don't go outside."

"Why would I go outside!?" Then Felicity heard the guests drive up to the cabin. "The family is back. Maybe they will scare it away."

"Get them in the house quickly. Get the rifle out and keep it handy."

Greg taught Felicity well how to shoot both of the guns and she expertly loaded the gun, set the safety on and placed it up high on a shelf, but within easy reach. She went to the front door and waited for the family to begin getting out of their car. She opened the front door. "Quickly now, come! Get inside!"

They were laughing and joking but the mother looked concerned, so she picked up her little daughter and shooed her teens into the house.

"Is there a problem?" The father asked.

"There's just a bit of wildlife activity out and about. Come on, quickly get inside."

The man obeyed but seemed amused with her concern. That was until a big black creature came crashing through the tree line. This propelled him into the house, and he stood over his children and wife.

Just then Greg's truck came rumbling into the clearing. The headlights illuminated the creature as he turned sharply in the clearing to scare it off.

Felicity had never been so relieved to see a bear. The bear turned tail and ran back into the trees frightened by Greg's truck as he intended.

Greg honked the horn and shouted out the window for good measure to ensure the old bear was too scared to come back.

He ran up to the house and Felicity let him in, quickly shutting and deadbolting the door behind them.

"Is everyone alright? It's just Harry. An old bear that comes through this way once a year. He doesn't usually bother people though. I'm going to call animal control and have them come check him out. He might be getting senile."

"I'm sorry for the excitement." Felicity said to her smiling yet trembling guests.

"No, no, it was quite exciting. I appreciate you looking out for us," the mother said.

"I've made you hot cocoa, it's already in the kitchen." The family thanked her and went off to enjoy their hot chocolate treat.

Greg took Felicity in his arms. "You probably think I'm such a dork." She said.

"Only a little." He used his fingers to show just how small. He squeezed her then pulled her by the hand into the hall by her bedroom.

"Listen, I didn't want to scare your guests, but I think something might have scared that bear into this area."

"You mean my boyfriend?"

"Yes. The Bigfoot one, not me."

"You think he's back?"

"I don't know but it's not like Harry to go crashing through people's yards like that. I've seen that bear a hundred times wandering around the forest and he doesn't ever do more than waddle on his way and ignore me."

"Will you stay here tonight."

"Of course." He hugged her again. Then the father came into the hallway.

"Oh, excuse me." He said as he caught them in an intimate situation.

"I'll stay here tonight just in case there's any more trouble. I don't want to scare your family, but bears can easily rip a door off the frame if they want to get in."

"Well, that's fine with me. Did you call animal control yet?"

"No, I'll do that right now." Greg said, and he went into Felicity's room and shut the door behind him.

"Well, I've lived here for a few months and I've never had any trouble so don't worry about it. Greg is just a precaution. You know where to find me if you need anything. Good night."

Greg slept on the couch that night and Felicity couldn't sleep. She couldn't stop thinking about something busting through the door and attacking her. She got up and crept to the living room. The moonlight beamed through the cracks in the curtains and Felicity could make out Greg's form on the couch, just barely. She could hear his heavy breathing and see him twitch occasionally. She took the cushions off and climbed over the back, snuggling up next to Greg. He moved a little but quickly returned to his heavy and steady breathing which sent a ripple of calm over her and she fell fast asleep.

In the morning Greg woke up to the sound of little snores in his ear. He rolled over to see Felicity's dreamy face. Her black eyes had completely gone away and the gash on her forehead was just a pink scar now. He wondered how and when she got there. She must have been scared after the incident with the bear last night. Felicity moved a little and fluttered her eyes open.

"Hi." She tittered softly. "I couldn't sleep, and you are like wine."

"I wouldn't know, I don't drink wine." He said matching her quiet softness.

"Neither do I." She laughed lightly again.

He stroked her shining hair and kissed her forehead. "If I had known I would have slept in the chair in your room."

"I know. That's why I came out here, so you could actually sleep."

"I can sleep anywhere, actually."

"I believe it." She tried twisting and rubbed her lower back. "This couch is not ideal."

"I think it's a pretty good one." He kissed her forehead again and they heard a knock on the door.

Felicity gingerly climbed over Greg to answer the door. "Who in the dickens could it be?"

"Are you expecting guests?"

"I hope not, I'm not ready for them if I am."

Felicity opened the door a crack.

"I can't believe it!" She said as she threw open the door and Greg saw a handsome, thin, tall man standing in the door with his hands outstretched.

Chapter Eight

Greg and Felicity sat snuggled together on the roof watching the sunrise. It was their new daily ritual. Greg would show up, let himself in, and they would grab a tea and sit in perfect stillness as they took in nature and the warming glow of the rising sun.

"How's your guest?"
"He's good. I've got another couple coming today. They are taking the bunk room with a few kids." Felicity returned to her silent meditation.
"That's great. So, are you and David catching up a lot?"
"Kinda, he's divorced now, which is weird because I never thought he would divorce Sophie. They seemed like the perfect couple."
"How did he show up here of all places?"
"Oh, funny story. My mom posted the B&B listing on Facebook and he saw it, thought he needed a vacation, you know, after his divorce, and he drove all the way up here without booking."
"Why? Why would he drive up here without knowing if the room was available or not?"
"Good question. I guess people do desperate things after something like a divorce, right?"
"Yeah. I guess." Greg said as Felicity went back to her quiet meditation, but after a few moments Greg couldn't leave it alone. "I just think it would have been more polite for him to call, or book online. I mean, you've got to be prepared for guests."
"It worked out fine though. It's fine. I'm not mad about it."
"Wow!" David gasped as he popped his head out the window.
Startled, Felicity turned around, "Oh, David, good morning."
"Hey David." Greg waved unenthusiastically.

My Bigfoot Boyfriend

"I heard talking so I followed it and, wow! I can see why you two are hiding out here. I'm not interrupting, am I?"

"A little," Greg said at the same time Felicity said, "no."

"Good. I love this. That is the most beautiful view I've ever seen. Oh, wow!"

"So, David, what brings you up to the Pacific Northwest?"

"Freedom!" David shouted. Felicity giggled and Greg nodded skeptically.

"And what are you going to do when you are done vacationing?" Greg asked.

"I am not sure. I have three beautiful children and no job... I quit. My boss was not supportive of my divorce, she preferred that I work myself to death and not take care of my family."

"I quit my job for the same reason! Except for the kids' part." Felicity enthused.

"It's like, I feel lighter now, you know?"

"Yeah, I do!"

"I don't have any money," David laughed, "but I feel like I can conquer the world."

"What about those kids of yours?" Greg inquired.

"Their mom has them well in hand. For now. She's the one who wanted the divorce, so I figure she deserves any fall out because of it, you know?"

"You are just going to abandon your ex-wife and kids?" Greg balked.

"Greg!" Felicity shot him a disapproving look. "Give him a break, he just got divorced, it's not the end of the world if he takes a few weeks to find himself."

"Thank you Ellie. That's what I thought too. Divorce is hard, and it really takes a toll on a guy."

"Yeah, I'm sure it does, David." Felicity patted him on the back in a friendly way. He smiled warmly at her.

"So, when I saw your mom post about this little slice of heaven I just got in the car and didn't look back. Plus, bonus, I get to hang out with my old friend, Felicity— And meet your boyfriend." He added as an afterthought.

"Well, I've got to get back to my place and get some things done." Greg said nonchalantly as he pecked Felicity on the mouth.

"See you at lunch?"

"Uh, probably not today. I've got a lot to take care of. Dinner probably." Then he walked to the edge of the roof and bent over, put his left hand on the roof and jumped off.

"Wow." David blinked. "That was really cool."

Felicity smiled. "Yeah, he's pretty dreamy."

"That was like *Tom Cruise* cool."

"Yeah, okay." Felicity laughed. "I better get breakfast ready before the Sokolowski's are up.

"I'd love to help, if that's not against some policy at the... Do you have a name for this place?"

"Uh, no. Should I?"

"I think it would make it sound even cooler than it is."

"Ok, well it was my uncle Ben's place."

"That sounds like a restaurant. What about Ben's Lodge?"

"Sounds good to me." Felicity smiled.

"Great, so any policy at Ben's Lodge against a guest helping with breakfast?"

"No. Come on, I'll let you bake the muffins."

"That's probably ill advised, but I will give it my best shot."

"Well why are you volunteering if you suck at cooking?" Felicity asked as she climbed back into the loft. David followed.

"The company of course."

"Well, in that case, I'll do my best not to swear at you when you burn the muffins."

"Yes, *Chef*, yes!"

"Ah, Devil Chef!"

"That's the one!"

"I love-hate that show."

"I know right?"

David and Felicity created a successful, not burnt breakfast of biscuits and gravy, muffins, and eggs with bacon that the Sokolowski children barely touched.

"Don't take it personally," David soothed as he put his arm around Felicity as she was putting away the leftovers. "It's just kids, there was nothing wrong with your cooking."

"Oh, I know. I'm fine. At least I don't have to cook lunch!" She laughed lightly.

"Hey, are there any good hikes up here?"

"Yes, of course, the best in the country. Probably."

"Ha! Well, what do you say? Pack a lunch and take a hike?"

Felicity wanted to say yes but her mind was registering some reservations. One, you are with Greg and this sounds like a date. Two— no, there is just that one big one. David was being all too friendly for a guy who just got divorced and knew she had a boyfriend.

"That sounds great! But I've got so much to do around here. This place has got to stay perfectly clean."

"Well, I may not be much of a cook, but this guy can clean." He pointed at himself with his thumbs.

"David—"

David's face fell, "I'm sorry, if you don't want to go you can just be straight with me."

"It's not that I don't want to go, it's more like I feel like we need to have an understanding."

"Oh, this is about Greg?"

"Yeah."

"He's a jealous type, huh? I get it, he doesn't like you having guy friends."

"I don't think that's it, it's more the understanding between us that we are friends."

"What? You thought this was like, what? A date? Felicity! This is—" He pointed between the two of them back and forth, "just friends. Okay? I just got divorced, I'm not ready to jump into anything right now, not even dating."

"Okay, I'm sorry. I just wanted to be clear."

"No, no! I get it, It's nothing. No worries. So, are we going?"

"Yeah! But first—"

"What?"

"The broom and mop are in that pantry cupboard over there."

"Right. On it."

"How did you and Greg meet?" David asked as he stepped over a log on the trail.

"It's a long story." Felicity was in no way going to tell David what really happened, that a Bigfoot was chasing her, and she tripped over a log and Greg rescued her. "In short, he is my neighbor and he knew my uncle. He came to my assistance when I first got into town."

"And how long have you been in town, how long have you been together?"

"It was late February when I moved here and now it's late May. Nearly three months. Time flies."

"Yeah, but it's not been that long, how much of that time have you been together?"

"Most of it, I guess, it took us a few weeks to get on the same page, but we've essentially been together ever since the first week."

"I was with Sophie for eight years."

"I know. I'm sorry. You seemed like the perfect couple."

"We were. That's what is so hard about it. She just up and got divorce papers one day. She said that she wasn't *made for married life.*"

"Do you think she was cheating on you?"

"I don't know. I didn't see any signs but why else would you throw eight beautiful years and a family of five out the window?"

"That's rough, David."

"Yeah, well. Oh well! You live, you learn. Hey, remember that time we went to Havasu for graduation? That was a fun trip."

"Yeah, I remember."

"You turned me down on that trip."

"I know."

"I'll bet you are regretting it now." David laughed. "I mean, before you got with Greg."

"To be honest, I've thought about you a lot over the years. I've watched you online, with your happy family and wondered if that could have been me." Felicity remarked.

"Maybe if it was, you and I would still be happily married, and you wouldn't have left me with no explanation." David answered.

"Maybe. But you know, I don't know how my life would have fit into yours. I went to college for four years and I've been working sixty-hour work weeks for years. I wouldn't have been able to do that and have kids. I probably would have been a terrible wife and mother."

"I think we could have made it work. You probably wouldn't have felt the need to work so much if you had a family."

"I never thought about it that way. Here we are——" Felicity stated as they hiked around one last corner, David could see why Felicity brought him here. The trees cleared and there was a beautiful meadow covered in wildflowers in the middle. From the clearing you could see the same mountain range they were admiring this morning on the roof.

"Wow! That is really something! It's like a fairytale." David exclaimed.

They walked in silence to the middle of the meadow and just looked around and took in the beauty.

"I've actually never been here. Greg told me he was going to take me here soon, when we had a quiet day at the lodge." said Felicity.

"This is exactly what I needed today." David said as he put an arm around Felicity. She looked up at him and smiled.

"Good, I'm glad I could help."

David's eyes searched Felicity's face. "I wish it was you. I thought about you a lot over the years too. I always felt like you were the one who got away."

Felicity swallowed hard and looked away. She walked herself out from under his arm.

"Oh look, a lupine!" She bent over and picked up the purple cone shaped flower. "I thought they were all done for the year. Lucky." David walked over and picked a red satin flower, he turned to Felicity and tucked it behind her ear. "We better head back," She said as she checked her watch. "I've got to get the beds turned down for the other guests."

"I don't want to miss another opportunity." He said quietly and stepped even closer, gently taking her elbow. Felicity's heartbeat was now roaring in her ears. She had thought about this for years and now it was actually happening, and she could only think about Greg.

"Come on, let's go." Felicity turned away from David and began to walk away, hoping her answer was clear.

She stayed pretty well away from David as they hiked back, and she was glad it was downhill, and she could keep a super-fast pace. But as she got close to the bottom of the trail, she heard a rustling and a deep growl in the woods. She froze and listened.

"What's the matter?" David asked as he jogged to catch up with her.

"Shhh…" He froze as he could hear it too.

Felicity nodded at David to keep going. And they both slowly crept a bit further down the trail. Then they heard a crashing in front of Felicity, and out jumped a tall figure. The adrenaline that shot through her body caused her to strike out at the attacker. She swung a punch and hit him squarely in his jaw.

"Connor! So, help me! You…" She used every swear word she could think of and Connor laughed as he held his jaw. A lady in a white track suit covered in leaves came out of the bushes next. Then Felicity realized she had backed up into David's arms and he was holding her. She ignored it for the moment.

"I'm sorry Felicity!" Connor laughed. "I didn't know I would scare you so bad! When I saw you coming down the trail, I just thought I'd play a little joke on you!"

"Connor, you scared me really bad."

"Hey, I'm Connor." He held out his hand and David shook it.

"David."

"Cool, where's Greg, Felicity?"

"He's at home. David's a guest and old friend."

"Ah, nice to meet you, man." Connor took his unknown girlfriend by the hand and they waved as they went up the trail, leaving Felicity still in David's arms. She tried to get away, but he held her tightly.

"David, I—"

"I just want you to hear me out."

"Ok." Felicity relented and turned around to face him.

"You are the only girl I've ever dreamed about. The truth is, Sophie and I got along fine, but I don't think we ever connected the way you and I do."

"David, that was high school. Surely we are both so different now."

"I'm not going to let you get away from me again."

"Really this is just your emotions from the divorce talking."

David pulled her in so close there was no getting away and he put his hand on the back of her head guiding her into a kiss. She didn't reciprocate the kiss and she kept her lips tight and unyielding.

After a moment David realized he was not going to get kissed back and let go of her.

"Not cool, David!" Felicity said as she stomped off, nearly back to the lodge.

"I'm sorry!" He chased after her. "Felicity, I'm sorry!"

When Felicity got back to the cabin Greg was just coming up to the house.

"Hey!" He smiled but Felicity walked past him into the cabin. Greg saw David run up shortly after. He seemed embarrassed and wouldn't look Greg in the eye.

"Felicity, wait!"

A moment later Felicity came out with a suitcase, barely closed and threw it in the driveway.

David followed after her again.

"You are not welcome here." And she turned around and went back inside. Greg folded his arms over his chest.

"Bye, David." He chuckled as he let himself in and locked the door behind himself. "Hey babe." He said as he found Felicity sitting on the edge of her bed.

"You knew this morning somehow, didn't you? That's why you were acting so weird with David."

"I knew what? What happened?"

"He wanted to go on a hike, as friends. Then he relentlessly put the moves on me until he was able to lock me in a kiss that I didn't want!"

"Oh. Yeah, I knew he was trying to put a wedge between us. I didn't think he would be dumb enough to try anything like that." Greg got up for what Felicity assumed was to kick David's backside.

"No, Greg!" He turned around. "I need you." Felicity sighed and held out her arms. "Just let him leave in peace."

Greg came over and wrapped his arms around her and pulled her into a cuddle on the bed, holding her tightly. He kissed her head and held her until they both fell asleep.

Chapter Nine

"Welcome to Ben's Lodge!" Felicity chimed as her new guests, a couple in their thirties walked through the front door. "Greg will help you with your bags and show you your room, here is your room key and one to the front door. Breakfast is at eight am." Greg smiled and winked at her before he picked up most of their bags and showed them to one of the queen bedrooms.

"They seem nice." He said as he returned to Felicity's side.

"Yes, so they are all settled in then? Connor is bringing some chick here tonight, I'm not sure why I agreed to it, but we have the space so I can't really say no, can I?"

"Be patient with Connor, he just went through a bad breakup with his wife."

"You mean like you were patient with David?"

"Connor didn't force you to kiss him."

"Yet." Felicity smirked.

"Well he better not. I'd hate to have to kick his—"

"Okay, I get it." Felicity laughed. "You have nothing to worry about. You are the only guy for me."

"Damn straight!" He said before kissing her. Then he kissed her nose and made his way down to her neck.

"Greg!" Felicity laughed, "That tickles."

"Oh really?" He said, as he then began to dig his fingertips into her ribs.

"Ah! Stop it!" She giggled.

"Erghhm." They heard from the direction of the front door and stopped their folly to look at who had interrupted them. It was Connor and yet another girl Felicity had never seen before.

"Hey, Connor!" Greg said as he let go of Felicity. Felicity could swear that she saw the new girlfriend of Connors roll her eyes. Then she knew why, "Hey Ginger! I didn't know you were dating! That's great!"

"Hey Greg. I didn't know you were dating anyone either." She said, not able to keep the contempt in her voice in check, but Greg didn't seem to notice.

"Sorry guys, Greg, you wanna grab their bags? Your room is right this way and here are your keys. One for the front door and one for your room." Felicity showed them to their room only to be met with more vitriol from Ginger.

"Wait there's no bathroom!"

"There's a community bathroom down the hall." Felicity said as politely as she could muster given Ginger's tone of voice.

"Okay, wow. Nice place Connor."

"Enjoy your stay." Felicity said as she ducked out of the room and shut the door behind her. Then she realized that Greg was still in there as he came out a moment later.

"Don't worry about Ginger, she's quite the firecracker but she's a good person."

"You say that about everyone. I wonder if you think axe murderers are good people too."

"Well, it depends on why they murder." Greg smiled.

"Oh, saved by the bell." Felicity said as the doorbell rang, the final guests for the night had arrived. When she opened the door, she noticed that it had started to get windy and the sky had darkened significantly. "Looks like a storm is rolling in, Greg."

"Yeah, I think I heard that we are expecting a big summer thunderstorm tonight on the news."

"Do you think it will be okay?"

"What?"

"The storm, do they get bad here?"

"Oh yeah. It's going to be a night to remember."

"Great." Felicity said flatly as she opened the door. "Welcome to Ben's Lodge!"

This was an older couple in their sixties, dressed in their best outdoor gear, ready to go fishing and hiking as soon as possible.

Felicity handed them their keys and had Greg show them to their room. When he returned, they picked up where they left off. Greg pulled her in close and picked her up off the ground so he could kiss her without craning either of their necks.

"Erghm." Connor said as he and Ginger came into the room.

"Do you guys need a room?" Ginger asked.

"I was just wondering if I could take Ginger out on the roof."

"Oh, yeah sure." Felicity smiled.

"Just be careful, a lightning storm is coming in." Greg added.

Connor and Ginger passed them as they headed up the stairs to the loft. Greg picked up Felicity again and this time he traced the outline of her lips with his softly before he kissed her when, BANG. Thunder clapped above their heads sending Felicity's heart rate through the roof.

Greg squeezed her tighter as he put her down and they laughed at themselves for jumping.

"Woo!" Connor said as he came down the stairs with Ginger. "Forget that, that's a nasty storm." Just as he finished speaking two more claps of thunder exploded.

"Well, this is going to be a fun night! I love thunderstorms!" Greg clapped his hands once and then rubbed them together. "I'm going to start a fire! The power is probably going to go out."

"Great." Ginger said angrily.

The older couple came out of their room. "Wow, that's quite the storm we got!" the man said. "Mind if we watch it from the porch?"

"Not at all, that should be safe."

They headed out to the front porch and sat on the Adirondack chairs.

"I brought dinner!" Connor chirped as he went off to his room and then returned with a casserole dish and a grocery bag. "We talked about getting together and we never did, so I thought, why not tonight?"

"Great!" Felicity did not relish the idea of having to sit down with Ginger and have to endure her sneers all night long, but she was a five-star rated host and she was going to be the best dang host in spite of Ginger's bad attitude.

They sat at the kitchen table together after Greg grabbed some plates and silverware and Felicity grabbed a few cups and drinks.

"No worries, I didn't cook this myself!" Connor laughed as he set the casserole dish on the table and removed the tinfoil lid. "I had Joey at the diner make this for us tonight and I brought a boysenberry pie."

"We should have you over more often!" Greg said, practically drooling over the casserole.

"What is it?" Ginger said with a sneer.

"It's some sort of Mexican casserole, he swore we would love it."

"It smells amazing!" Felicity said as she began to dish up everyone around the table.

"Thanks for bringing dinner Connor, we really should do this more often." Greg said just before he shoved a huge bite into his mouth.

Ginger rolled her eyes. Felicity hoped that Ginger wasn't the one girlfriend that stuck for Connor.

"Where did you two meet?" Felicity asked as she poured herself a drink.

"We met through Greg." Connor said after he swallowed a big bite.

"Yeah, I know Ginger from—"

"We dated." Ginger said with that same sneer on her fake lips, again.

"Oh. Well, small world out here in the middle of nowhere."

"Yeah, I met Ginger on an online dating app a year or so ago. Back when I tried those sorts of things."

"He stopped calling me." Ginger said flatly with almost no emotion on her face, except a twitching eyebrow.

"Sorry Ginger, I thought it was mutual."

"Well, it's water under the bridge." Connor said as he poured himself a large drink. Before he could fill his glass, the lights went out.

"Told ya. I'll go see if I can get it back on. It's probably not anything we can fix. These electrical storms take out the whole grid sometimes. Feliss, there's some flashlights, matches and candles in that drawer by the fridge.

Felicity carefully made her way to the counter and felt around for the drawer. She felt a flashlight and flipped it on so she could find some candles too.

"Here you go." She said as she handed Greg the flashlight and then lit the candle.

"Be right back," he said.

"Don't touch me." Ginger said to Connor. *Why is she even here with him?* Felicity thought.

"Here's a candle for you, I'm going to go check on my other guests."

Felicity first went to check on the couple on the porch. "You guys okay out here?"

"Oh yes, we are fine, I see we've lost power though."

"Yes, we have. Greg is looking to get it back on but if he doesn't, I can hook you up with a flashlight and a candle."

"Alright, we'll go inside now." The husband said as they got up. Felicity handed them a few matches and a candle and as they came inside the younger couple came out of their room.

"Is the power out?" the wife asked, her bright blonde hair practically glowing in the faint light.

"Yeah, are you guys okay?"

"Why would they be? This is the worst B&B ever." Ginger snapped from the kitchen.

Felicity let it pass. Hopefully Ginger wouldn't leave a review. "Here's a match and a candle."

Felicity held the candle low so she could see over it. She wondered where Greg was. It shouldn't take him that long to check out the power box. More lightning, nearly one every second shook the house.

The young wife had a grasp on her husband's arm. "You're digging into my arm Franny!" He complained.

Then the sounds of heavy rain pounding the ground started far off and got closer and closer, followed by a heavy wind. The older couple must not have shut the front door all the way because it flew open followed by a spray of rainy wind that put out all of their candles. This made the younger woman scream out in fear. Felicity jumped thinking at first that someone, or something had kicked the door in. She rushed over the best she could in the dark and shut the door. Making sure it was closed tightly, then locked it for good measure.

"Here," she said as she struck another match and lit a candle, passing a light-giving gift around to everyone else.

"This is the worst—" Ginger began but was interrupted by more thunder. Felicity had a good idea what she was saying.

The continuous thunder put the younger wife more and more on edge. She began to almost whimper.

"Hey, it's going to be okay, Franny." Felicity tried to comfort her, but she was beginning to worry herself about Greg. He should be back inside by now; he should know if he could get the power back on by now. "I'm going to go check on Greg." She said as she got another flashlight from the drawer and threw on a coat.

Outside the rain was coming down in sheets that were occasionally illuminated by the lightning. Her face was being pelted by the droplets being hurled at her by the wind. "Greg!" She called out but it didn't matter, every time she tried to yell for him the thunder out sang her by decibels.

"Greg!" No sign of him by the electrical box. Where could he be? She worried something happened to him. What if he got struck by lightning? Or a certain Bigfoot boyfriend of her's nabbed him. "Greg! Where are you?" She called again.

She turned the next corner of the house and ran straight into a lumbering figure. She screamed but the thunder overpowered it.

The figure grabbed her by the arms. "It's me!"

"Greg?"

"No Connor!"

"Oh, Connor you scared me! What are you doing out here?"

"I'm helping you!"

"Well, did you see him?"

"No, I wonder if he went home?"

"Why would he do that?"

"Maybe he needed some tools? I don't know! Why would any guy ever leave you?"

Felicity paused and tried to look up at Connor, but the rain was falling too hard. He grabbed her hand and pulled her up close to him. "Listen! I-" but his words were lost in the thunder.

"What? I can't hear you!"

"I really want you—"

Well, that was more than enough for her to hear. "Connor, no!"

"Yes! I want to—" But more thunder. Then he pulled her in and kissed her, but she didn't wait to squirm away from him. She went into the house. Connor sighed and swore a few times. He really blew it. He thought that kissing out in the rain would be romantic, but it really wasn't, then he turned around to an angry Greg standing on the porch.

"I'll deal with you in a minute." Greg growled as he went in the house.

"Greg! There you are! I was looking for you!"

"I got this message this morning. I disregarded it until I just walked up to you kissing Connor on the porch just now." Greg handed her his phone and there was a text message from an unknown number on it. It read:

Felicity is cheating on you.

"Every time I turn around, I find you kissing or hanging on another guy."

"Greg, I had nothing to do with it!"

"Who did he kiss?" Ginger squealed as Connor walked in, the wind blowing out the candles again.

"I just walked up on these two kissing on the porch." Greg said calmly pointing an accusatory beam of light from his flashlight at each of them.

"You pig!" Ginger snapped and smacked Connor across the face. "I was going to give you a weekend you wouldn't forget!"

"Ginger, Greg, I'm sorry." Connor said and then he disappeared into the dark.

"Greg, I'm not cheating on you I swear."

"You know, the truth is I don't know you that well. And I've seen you lead on two different men to the point where they thought they could kiss you."

"Greg, now hold on! I didn't mislead anyone. I made sure that David understood that you and I were together, and Connor is just, well... Connor!" The two guest couples had slowly backed away from the fight and were hanging out in the kitchen. Felicity noticed the kitchen was glowing from their candles.

"I love you, Greg! You are the greatest thing that's ever happened to me! I would never do anything to screw this up!"

"Actions speak louder than words." Greg said and then he stormed out the door into the dark of night. Felicity watched as a few lightning bolts lit up the night enough that she could see him blip in and out as he walked away to his truck, then drove away, skidding out as he left.

"Sorry everyone. Goodnight." She said as she went to her room and locked the door behind her. There went her five-star rating and her five-star boyfriend.

The next morning the storm had completely run its course and Felicity could hear birds chirping and water dripping from the roof. She hoped that Connor and Ginger had left last night and then she would only have to contend with the couples that she didn't know.

Usually this time of the day she would be snuggled up next to Greg on the roof watching the sun come up. But he was not there.

She went to the kitchen and started the bacon and biscuits, then she scrambled some eggs while simultaneously cutting up a melon.

Once breakfast was cooked, she put it in chafing dishes and went to wake up the guests.

"Breakfast." She said as she knocked lightly.

She left out a pile of plates and silverware as well as some serving spoons and left the guests to fend for themselves as she went back to her room.

After three days of no Greg, him not answering his door or phone, Felicity had given up. She cancelled all of her bookings for the week and intended to spend the time sitting on the couch eating ice cream and precooked bacon.

She was a mess. Her hair was dirty, she had on old sweats and her face was red and blotchy from crying. It was not a great time for someone to knock at the door. They persisted even though she ignored it for quite some time. Finally, when the bell ringing began to be a constant, she got up and threw open the door.

"David! What are you doing here?"

"Ellie, are you okay?"

"I'm fine, what do you want?"

"I'm sorry to come back here but I think I left my dad's ring here. It's really important to me and I needed to come back for it."

"You could have texted me an address to send it to."

"I was still in the area so I thought it would be better if I came to look for it myself."

"Okay, fine. Come in." Felicity stood aside as David came in and started toward the room, he had stayed in. He began looking under the bed and tables.

"I haven't seen it, and I clean these rooms thoroughly." She said as she stood in the doorway watching his every move.

"I'm going to go check in the bathroom." He squeezed past her in the doorway as she was unwilling to move, looking grumpy and put out.

"Are you sure you are okay?" He said as he began looking around the floor of the bathroom.

"Yeah, why?"

"You seem... Depressed?"

"Greg left. I haven't heard from him in days. Won't return my calls."

"I'm sorry."

"I'll bet you are, it's mostly your fault. He thinks I'm a 'loose woman' because you and Connor both tried to kiss me and got caught."

"Connor tried to kiss you?"

"Yeah, idiot."

"Well, you are— Irresistible."

"Not again, David. Please."

"Felicity, I don't mean to sound like an opportunist but, if it weren't for Greg what would have happened between us?"

"I don't know."

"Ellie, look at me." She didn't want to, she just wanted to be angry at him. He gently put a hand under her chin. "Ellie, we would be together. You and I have always had an undeniable connection. First, Sophie got in the way and then Greg. Now, we have a chance.

"I still have hope for Greg, David. It's not like he's going to be gone forever, he is just mad right now, and then when we talk and he realizes that nothing happened on my end he will forgive me and we can move on."

"Okay, fair enough." David said. "But I don't want to lose you as a friend. I lost half of my friends in the divorce and I can't lose one more. Especially such an old one."

"We can be friends then. Just promise me you won't try anymore moves!"

"Scouts honor." He saluted.

"That's not how you do it."

He shrugged. "I was never a scout"

"Obviously. Come on, I have way more ice cream than I should be eating alone, and I hate watching Gilmore Girls by myself."

"I love Gilmore Girls." He said as he settled into the couch. "You don't have any guests?"

"No, I cancelled all the ones I had this week."

"Looks like I got here just in time then. You need someone to pull you back

on your feet."
"Fine, but after I finish season Five."
"What episode are you on?"
"One."

Chapter Ten

"Any word from Greg?" David asked as he helped himself to some juice in the fridge the next morning. "And, thanks again for letting me stay last night. I didn't realize how much I needed a night of the Gilmore Girls too."

"No, nothing yet. I hope he's okay. I'm really worried about him. Do you think he's overacting?"

"Yeah, totally. He should believe you when you say you didn't instigate the kissing."

"I wish he did."

"Well, let's not dwell on Greg today, I'm here to help you out and get you back on your feet. Let's get this place cleaned up, get the fridge stocked. You have bookings for next week?"

"Yeah a few. I was hoping Greg would be—"

"Nope, Let's not think about Greg today. Let's focus on you and your business, okay?"

"You are right, I can't let my whole life crumble because Greg is mad at me."

"Exactly. I'll start on the bedrooms and you can work here." David said as he put a sympathetic arm on her shoulder as he passed her.

David was being really great and for a moment Felicity let herself think about what it would be like with him here instead of Greg. Then she remembered his forceful hand on the back of her head, pushing her into an unwanted kiss and she frowned to herself. She felt like that was perhaps, a big red flag... But as long as he behaved, they should be fine.

After a long day of cleaning, Felicity was tired and just wanted to sit on the couch again and watch season six of Gilmore Girls. She plopped herself down on the sofa with a pint of cookie dough ice cream and began digging around for just the dough in the carton.

David was in the shower and she had no intention of showering because she didn't feel like it and maybe it would offer some protection to his advances. He had done well the whole day though, not flirting or acting cute in any way. She still desperately missed Greg though. Nothing she did all day filled the hole of not seeing his face and hearing his laugh.

It was getting dark and she pulled a blanket over herself, even though it wasn't cold. She stuck her feet out so she wouldn't be too hot. Then she must have fallen asleep. The next thing she knew, she was waking up to the sound of the front door opening. At first, she thought it might just be David leaving, then she realized that David was sleeping next to her on the couch. He had laid down next to her and fallen asleep. Then who was at the door?

"Felicity?" It was Greg's voice.

"Greg!" She said as she popped up off the couch and ran to him. "Where have you been? I've been so worried!"

She swung her arms around his neck and kissed him everywhere on his face.

"Oh, hey Greg." David said as he sat up on the couch.

Felicity felt Greg's body stiffen and she unwrapped her arms from around him.

"Obviously you weren't that worried." Greg said as he stepped back toward the door.

"Thanks a lot David! Get out of here for good this time!"

"Felicity, if he doesn't believe you, he's not worth it!" He yelled after her as she followed Greg out the door.

"Greg, wait. Greg." He didn't stop. She was able to catch up to him before he reached the treeline and grabbed his hand. "Greg, stop."

"There's nothing to be said, Felicity."

"Yes there is a lot to say! I didn't cheat on you, not once I never led anyone else on and I never allowed David to sleep next to me on the couch! This has all just been one unfortunate misunderstanding after another! I love you Greg! You are the only man in the world for me and you always will be. Please, trust me. If you love me, you need to trust me!"

Greg settled down slightly and took a deep breath. "Who sent me the text, that you are cheating on me?"

Felicity thought for a moment when it dawned on her. "Let me see it." Greg handed her his phone from his pocket and opened the message. She looked at the phone number.

"That's a California number."

"So?"

"So, it's probably David. He showed up right after you left and has been the perfect gentleman until he snuggled up to me on the couch without me knowing it."

"What about Connor?"

"You know I don't like Connor. You know it!"

Greg sighed. "I know. And you don't have any residual feelings for David?"

"No! In fact, I'm starting to seriously think he's a psychopath."

"Come here!" Greg said as he pulled her in close and squeezed her tightly.

"I missed you so much, don't you ever leave me again."

"I missed you too. I came back because I was going to forgive you for everything and anything because I love you so much. Finding you sleeping with another man was too much though."

"I know, that idiot. Should we call the police? He isn't even paying this time!"

"No, let me handle him." Greg said before he gently placed his parted lips on hers.

Before Greg and Felicity could get back to the house, they heard a car peeling out of the driveway, throwing rocks and dirt as it went. David left in a hurry. "Hopefully he'll never come back!" Felicity laughed while Greg snuggled her into him.

Chapter Eleven

The air started to get a chill and Felicity knew that winter was just around the corner. She and Greg had spent a glorious summer together. Every day they took walks and hikes around the forest, always discussing what it was they wanted their future to be. Greg dreamed of a slow life with a kid or two. He wanted opportunities to teach them how to do all the things he was good at and teach them at home as much as they learned at school. Felicity was happy just running the B&B for now but agreed she could fit some kids into her life if Greg wanted to. Greg was a very conservative person who hated all politicians and didn't care for most religions. He felt they were all two sides of the same hypocritical coin.

Greg often talked about a lot of things Felicity had never considered because she had been too busy working her whole adult life.

With fall starting, Felicity wanted to add fall activities to the lodge and so she arranged for pumpkins to be carved, Halloween movies to stock the cabinet with and she even splurged on some decorations that made the cabin look like it was straight out of a Good Housekeeping magazine for October.

On the matter of her Bigfoot boyfriend, she hardly thought about it anymore. She hadn't seen anything for ages, and she was too happy and preoccupied to worry about it.

One morning she heard Greg out around the back chopping firewood. She wanted to surprise him with coffee, so she went out the kitchen side door and rounded the cabin. To her horror she saw the hairy back of a Bigfoot hunched over the chopping block. She gasped and dropped the coffee cup on the ground. This got the creatures attention and it turned around.

Felicity took a minute to catch her breath as she made eye contact with Greg.

He jogged over to her. "What's the matter? What did you see?"

"You! What are you wearing?" She shrieked. Greg had a black furry bearskin coat on. "Greg! Are you my Bigfoot Boyfriend?"

"What?" He was confused and then looked down at his coat. "Huh." He finally said.

"Come inside, we have some things to talk about."

A million thoughts swirled through Felicity's mind. Greg was very tall, one of the tallest and most broad-shouldered men she had ever met.

"Not all of it makes sense though." Felicity calculated each instance in her head.

"You are telling me that all the times you thought you saw Bigfoot you think it was actually me?"

"I don't know, Greg. Tell me what happened the first week I arrived."

Greg's Story

It was a chilly and dark night with little moonlight. Greg was on his way back from the market after picking up some more propane and a few nonperishable food items for his off-grid cabin. He had recently lost a good friend of his, Ben, who lived a few cabins down the road from him and he was about to drive by his place. He saw a car parked on the side of the road just out front of Ben's turn off. It was a younger lady; he could tell by the size and shape of her frame. He thought he knew who it was. Ben's niece.

Ben had mentioned that he might leave his cabin to her. He didn't really know her and that made her the only family that he still liked. He recalled a conversation with Ben a year or so back.

Ben was taking Connor for all he was worth at poker that night and Connor wanted to up the ante.

"Listen Ben," Connor said in a drunken stupor, "I've got my place, I'll wager my place!"

"Your place!" Ben scoffed. "Your place doesn't hold a candle to mine! Why would I want your piddly little property? No, my friend, I'm cutting you off tonight!"

"No, come on Ben, be fair! Don't cut me off!"

"You're done, Connor!" Greg said, "the rule is when you start gambling away your car and house we are done!"

"Yup," Ben laughed. "And I am fair! I'll cut you out of the poker games as easily as I cut my sister and her simpering husband out of my will! No one's getting this place when I'm gone. I'm going to have it burned down instead, let nature take the property back."

Greg laughed, he knew Ben couldn't bear to see his cabin burned, even over his dead body. "Leave it to me!" He offered while he shuffled the cards and started dealing, but only to himself and Ben.

"No, no! I love you like a son, but you've got a great setup where you are at and I've got a sweet little niece who was raised by that moron of a brother-in-law that I want to leave it to. I'd hoped she'd want to live up here, but at the very least she could sell it. Maybe to you!" Ben laughed.

Back then when Ben mentioned his niece, Greg thought she was a little girl.

Ben was a bit of a cranky old fellow, especially since his longtime girlfriend left him a few years back. Greg didn't know her well, he couldn't even recall her name, but when she left Ben, it shook him to the core. Greg had thought over the past few months since he passed that it was due to too many years of a broken heart because Ben was fit and healthy. He hunted, hiked and took great care of himself otherwise, but the bitterness seemed to overtake him more and more as the years went on.

Greg pulled up to his little cabin, in the moonlight and after unloading his truck, he headed down the trail to Ben's place. The night was stiller than usual, as if the woods knew that there was a new arrival and was holding its breath to watch her. Greg noticed a faint smell of ozone in the air, likely a storm was rolling in.

As Greg got closer to Ben's he saw the girl go in the cabin through the side door. She looked nervous as she kept looking from side to side and slammed the door shut quickly behind her. Greg had worried that the power might be off, but a light flickered on quickly. He saw her stand in the middle of the kitchen looking around.

Greg stepped out of the trees in preparation to knock on the door and greet his new neighbor, but he got a glimpse of his reflection in the kitchen window. He had not shaved or cut his hair for many months and he looked positively wild. His beard was unseasonably long, and it blended into his bearskin jacket. He thought it best he not show up to her door in the dark like that and scare her half to death. He started to walk back towards the trail, crossing in front of the bedroom window as he went, he knew he shouldn't have but he couldn't help himself and he looked in the window. She was in bed trying to sleep. He didn't feel great about peeping but he was glad the poor girl was settled.

Greg woke the next morning before the sun. He couldn't sleep in anymore since basic training. He loved the morning, though. The air and the earth felt different in the morning than any other time of day. He lamented for those who were not morning persons because of the great beauty and tranquility they missed each day. After showering he considered shaving and cutting his hair to be presentable when he officially met Ben's niece. Just as he was about to start cutting, he got an alert on his phone.

WINTER STORM WARNING.

My Bigfoot Boyfriend

Greg checked the weather app on his phone. It was turning cold quickly and Ben's cabin often lost power when it snowed. It was easy enough to get it back on but there was no way that Ben's niece would know how to do this. *I need to get over there before too long and help her out with that.*

Greg had some things to do first to get his own cabin ready for the snow. It didn't snow much in this area, but this was supposed to be a big storm with freezing temperatures for days, and he was worrying about how Ben's niece would fare.

His roof tanks that he used for running water, might freeze and then leak if they were out in the freezing temps for too long. He would have to spend the day taking them down and hauling water into the house to use until the storm passed.

That evening after dark, he finally had a chance to head out to Ben's. As he walked the trail to Ben's, softly falling flakes began. The forest quieted as snow blanketed the ground and softened all sounds. He was now worried the girl would freeze to death as he felt the chill increasing in the air and the flakes grew in size and speed. As he came around the corner of Ben's he looked at the wood storage shed. It was empty. There were plenty of logs in the log pile, but none she would be able to get into the stove. *What were the chances this girl knew how to split wood? Not likely.* He thought he would split some wood for her and leave it there with some matches, just in case. He thought it might be kind of cute if she came out to see who was chopping and that is how they met for the first time. Then he remembered he never got around to shaving and the idea became less enchanting and he hoped she would *not* be interested to know.

He started chopping with Ben's old axe that he found leaning up against the cabin. It had been sitting out in the weather for a while and the head of the axe wasn't looking too good; the wood was looking a little loose. Greg got to work anyway; he was low on energy and didn't want to hike all the way back to his place two more times tonight to get his axe.

He chopped a few cords of wood before the axe head flew off the handle and hit the cabin. Greg winced as the impact almost made the logs ring. *Dang-it*, Greg thought. *Now I'm going to have to fix the axe.* He piled the wood he was able to finish under the shed.

Wait. what if she doesn't have any kindling? Greg had matches on him, but no kindling. He would just have to hope she had some papers inside she could use. He Left the matches on top of the shed, hoping she would see them.

He grabbed the axe head and shoved it back on the handle. It should hold well enough to carry it back to his place. By now he was covered in a light dusting of snow.

He was worried about the power going out but so far, the lights were still on inside. He'd have to wait until tomorrow to meet her. He needed to get the axe fixed so she would have firewood for tomorrow too, which promised to be equally as cold.

81

Greg started back on the trail up to his place. It was hard to see where the trail was since it was getting rapidly covered in snow and it was a very dark night. He would just have to do his best, but he stumbled, and the jolt made the head of the axe fall off the handle and it landed right on Greg's foot. It was a good heavy axe and even though he had heavy boots on, it happened to land on the least protected part of his foot. He let out a wail as he hopped around and mumbled some swears. It hurt more than it injured, thank goodness, but it left a bruise that made him limp slightly with every step.

Greg looked forward to another day that he could go meet his new neighbor. He had to admit he was intensely curious about her! But he wanted to get the axe done first. So, he passed the next day keeping warm in his cabin and working on fixing it. He had to make a new handle by whittling one that would fit. He didn't have any power tools, so he did it all by hand. It was a labor of love for his passed friend. Just as he finished and planned to take it back to Ben's place, he got a message from Connor.

Hey man, Ben's got a hot niece in town. She said her power's out and I won't make it till late, can you drop by and make sure she's okay?

Now Greg felt disappointed in himself. He knew her power would go out and yet he spent the day fixing the axe instead of checking on her. But he didn't want to show up empty handed. Greg hopped up and grabbed some tools he thought he might need, threw them in a pack and ran down to Ben's. He was coming up to the door when he heard the girl inside talking to someone about being hungry. He assumed that maybe she was on the phone.

Shoot. The poor thing didn't have any food in the place. He looked around the front and saw that her little car was snowed in and it looked like she tried to leave but she couldn't break free of a prison of snow.

Greg knew he didn't have much back at his place, but he could bring her a nice meal. He ran back to his place and grabbed some snacks and wrapped them in some eco-friendly paper—He didn't use plastic bags. He ran back down to Ben's and was about to knock on the front door when he saw his reflection again. He looked terrible. He had been running around in the snow all morning and he didn't want Ben's *hot* niece to see him this way. He thought he'd leave the package and get to work on getting the power back on.

He dropped the package on the front porch and walked over to the electrical panel on the back. *Damn!* Someone had put a combo lock on it. He'd have to go find some bolt cutters to get it off in order to get the power back on. He ran back to his place to search his shed. He thought he might have some but couldn't see them. He had lent them out to Bill, his neighbor down the other road and he'd have to go get them, so he jumped in his truck and headed to Bill's.

He knew Bill would keep him talking and he was ready for a quick exit. He knocked on Bill's door.

"Hey Bill! How are you man!" Greg said as Bill opened his door and smiled. Bill had a bit of a stoop and he reached out his hand for Greg to shake it.

"I'm well, Greg! How are you doing? You are looking like a real mountain man there!" Bill laughed at the sight of Greg's overgrown hair situation.

"I know, I know. Hey Bill, I'm wondering if you've still got my bolt cutters?"

Bill stopped and thought for a long minute. "You know, I can't recall. Let's go look in the shed."

"Alright!" Greg said politely but feeling the pressure of time weighing down on him.

"What are you up to in the middle of this cold snap?" Bill asked.

"Someone moved into Ben's, the powers gone out again and I'm trying to help but the damn realtor put a lock on the box."

"Oh, yeah. Those realtors are real shady. I don't trust them. When I sold five of my acres in Elk Point I just listed it in the paper." He said as he slowly walked to the shed.

Greg ran ahead and went to open the shed ahead of Bill, but it was locked.

"Hold on, young'un... I got to get a key." He mumbled as he patted all his pockets. "I've no key on me, I'll go fetch it in the house."

"Okay." Greg said as he painfully watched Bill slowly shuffle back to the house. A few minutes later Bill shuffled back out and to the shed.

"I sure am sorry about Ben being gone." Bill finally said as he fumbled with a massive handful of keys, trying to find the right one. "He was a good neighbor. Best damn hunter this county's ever seen too."

"Yeah, the best." Greg agreed. "He taught me best practices when I moved here. I sure miss him."

"Yeah." Bill grunted as he inserted a key into the shed's lock. It didn't fit. "I can't find the damn key, maybe it's on the other keyring." Bill started to shuffle back towards the house.

"You look tired, Bill, let me grab it for you. Where's it at?"

"I better do it. You'll never find it."

Greg took a deep breath and waited patiently for Bill to shuffle out again. This time he had a key separated from the rest. He put it in the lock, and it opened easily. He shuffled into the shed and fumbled for a light.

"There it is!" Greg said as he tried to squeeze past Bill to grab the cutters.

"Where?" Bill grunted as he tried to turn on the light, still.

Greg gently moved Bill over and bent over to pick up the cutters that were leaning up against an old rusty lawn mower in the shed that smelled like gas.

"I better be getting back." Greg said as he backed out of the shed.

"I- I-" Bill started with a shaky voice.

"Yeah Bill?" Greg stopped. He thought maybe Bill was having a stroke.

"I remember that year that the elk were passing through. It was the year, uh, let's see... The year that Anna... No, the year before Anna left Ben."

Anna! That was her name! Greg thought.

"I remember it well; it was the year I moved in."

"Yep, yep. Ben was happy then, remember. That was the last time he was, before that witch killed him."

Greg nodded solemnly but inside he was surprised with the turn that story had taken.

"She was always wanting more, and more and Ben, God rest his soul, he couldn't give it to her."

"Yes, it's unfortunate that Ben was so unhappy his last days."

"Unfortunate! That woman has as good as murdered him in my book."

"I can see why you would think-" Greg started but Bill interrupted.

"You stay away from loose women like that. She was a loose woman for sure. Anna had men all up and down this county, you know."

"Yeah, I'll bet she did." Greg indulged him. "I've really got to get going, Bill. It's been a pleasure visiting with you."

"Yeah, she was a real piece of work. Anna. Alright, you head on out now and charm the pants off of Ben's niece!" Bill laughed roughly then coughed and shuffled toward the house.

"Bill, you dog!" Greg laughed.

Bill just threw a dismissive hand at Greg and laughed to himself as he slowly went back into the house.

Greg drove back to his place and got back on the trail to Ben's place. As he came out of the forest, he saw that Connor's truck was there. He knew that even if Connor knew how to fix the power that he wouldn't be able to get into the panel. So, Greg went around and cut the lock and got to work fixing the problem.

Ben had shown him how to do it when they were playing poker one snowy night. They took turns going out, tightening up a few screws and flipping it back on. The weight of the snow on the lines and box would cause a short. It was pretty dangerous, and Greg thought he needed to make sure that Ben's niece had it fixed right away. He flipped the main power switch down, dusted off the snow and tightened everything back up when he flipped the switch back up the power turned on. He wanted to go talk to Ben's niece, but Connor was in there and he was one heck of a player, so he thought he better just be on his way.

As he was hiking back up the hill trail toward his place, he could hear Connor get in his truck shortly followed by the roar of his diesel engine rattling down the road. He thought maybe he would go back and introduce himself but as he headed back, he saw the tell-tale red glow of brake lights as her car left as well. He walked back to his place and got ready for bed before he texted Connor.

Got the power back on. Some numb nuts put a combo lock on it and had to find some bolt cutters. How is she?

She's great. A little young for me. Going out with Rhonda tonight. Wish me luck.

About thirty minutes later Connor texted again.

Just ran into her at the store with Rhonda. Think she likes me. Kind of awkward.

Good. I didn't want to have to tell her what a dog you are.

Connor didn't respond again even though Greg was just joking. Mostly.

He thought she might be on her way back and he wanted to make sure her car made it down the road safely and he also wanted to meet his new neighbor, finally! He got dressed and headed back down the trail again. Halfway down he realized that he still had not yet trimmed his beard, and he could have at least pulled his hair back. He hoped he wouldn't scare her to death. Just as he came out of the woods, he saw her getting bags out of her car, so he started to jog over to help her. He underestimated how rough he looked, because when she saw him coming at her she started screaming hysterically, jumped in her car and tried to back out of there as fast as she could.

While trying to turn the car around she backed the rear wheels into a muddy, ice spot and her tires were spinning out in the icy mud. Greg knew a trick, so he jogged over to help her out. If you pushed on the back of the car, the extra weight could help the tires gain enough traction to get out of the ruts they were making. He pushed on the trunk several times as hard as he could letting out grunts as he put all of his strength into it until the car took off. He ran after her to make sure she got out of the driveway ok then he watched as the car lost control through a puddle and ran off the road into a bush. The car made scraping and crunching sounds that made Greg wince, then he worried the airbags may have gone off and she might be incapacitated.

He ran down the road to make sure she was ok. She must have been because she jumped out of the car and started running. Greg didn't want to scare her further, but he was worried that she would get lost or hurt so he followed after her. She seemed strangely hysterical. He was much faster than she and he was about to call out to her to stop and that he was a friend of Ben's when she disappeared into tightly spaced trees. Greg couldn't run here, so he slowed down and stooped as he navigated his way through the woods. He pulled out his phone and turned on the flashlight app.

"Hey, I'm your neighbor from up the road! I'm sorry I scared you! I'm your uncle Ben's friend if that helps!"

Greg noticed something dark piled on the ground and shined his flashlight on it. It was her, crumpled, face down.

Greg rushed to her side and turned her over. She was out cold and had a gash on her head that was trickling blood. He picked her up and carried her back to her cabin. He looked down at her as they walked. Her head was bleeding on his bearskin jacket. He began to worry somewhat that when she woke, she might call the cops on him. He did just chase her through the woods. He had the best intentions, but she knocked herself out before she could discover that.

He kicked the front door open and took her to the back bedroom. He took off her coat and boots and put her in her bed. He found a first aid kit under the bathroom sink, and he tended to her head. She didn't appear to have a concussion, but she was still out cold. The only clinic didn't open any time soon and he thought she could wait. The gash on her head was not as bad as it looked but she had given herself two black eyes.

Greg stoked the fire she had already started and decided he should run back to his place to get his truck so he could pull her car out.

It wasn't easy, even with his four-wheel drive, her car had hi centered itself on a stump and didn't want to come free. Greg used a jack to get the car high enough to overcome the stump. It was a process of a lot of trial and error and took him the better part of an hour. When he went back in the house, Greg caught a glimpse of himself in the bathroom mirror as he walked by. He checked in on Ben's niece, still steady pulse, breathing fine, no signs of distress. This was his chance to get himself cleaned up before he met her, so he found an old shaving set of Ben's in the bathroom and trimmed his beard short and cut his hair. Then he took advantage of a warm shower and changed into some fresh clothes from his truck. It was about five AM and he heard the girl stir. He had been checking on her all night long. All of her vitals were good, and her pupils were responding normally to light. By six AM he could hear her stirring so he went to the room to introduce himself.

"Then you know the rest, because you were there." Greg said.

"So, you *were* the Bigfoot I saw peeping in my window that first night?"

"Yeah, sorry about that."

"And you were the one banging the wood around and hitting the cabin? And you left me the wood?"

"Yes, you are welcome."

"And you are the one who fixed the power and you didn't make it go out in the first place?"

"You are welcome and of course not!"

"And you left me the food?"

"Yeah, I had no idea you had ever seen me, and I didn't know you thought those things were done by a Bigfoot!"

"And that whole night you looked after me and you shaved and why do you wear that hideous coat that makes you look like a Bigfoot?"

"I found it at a thrift shop, it's really warm. And of course, I looked after you. It was my fault you crashed your car, and I wanted to make a good impression, so I cleaned myself up to meet you. Obviously, I scared you the first time you saw me, or the first time I thought you saw me, so I shaved."

"I don't know if I should laugh or cry!"

"Me neither. My girlfriend thinks I look like a big hairy monster!"

"Well, you did! You are really tall and with your hair and beard all wild, plus your long fur coat that is black— I thought you were hairy from head to toe!"

"I'm so sorry! I've caused you so much fear since you arrived!"

"Yes, you have! I'm just relieved that there's not really a Bigfoot though."

"Me too. I can sleep a lot easier when I'm not around, knowing that you aren't being stalked by anyone but me."

Felicity laughed and put her arms around Greg's neck. "I love my Bigfoot Boyfriend!"

"And he loves you." Greg whispered before placing a kiss on her lips.

It was a chilly December day, but Felicity and Greg didn't care. They loved their morning walks and would just bundle up when it got too cold. The rental season had all but closed down and they hadn't had a guest for quite some time, so they spent their days together getting to know one another. They fit together in a perfect way. Felicity felt complete before she arrived, but she felt whole when she was with Greg. And Greg never knew that being with someone could feel so much like having a home. He breathed in deeply as they rounded a dense grove of trees and took in the energizing smell of damp pine and soil. There was a light dusting of snow on the ground and he noticed a footprint. He walked up to it and studied it quizzically for a moment.

"Is it that old bear?"

"No. Greg said with confusion written on his face. "They had to put him down."

"Oh, I'm so sorry for him."

"Yeah." Greg said, distracted.

"Greg, what is it?" Felicity asked looking down at the print. "Huh," she laughed, "it looks like a giant human foot." Once the words came out of her mouth, she realized why Greg was confused.

"It's fine, it's probably just a bear print that's been distorted so it looks like a human foot."

"Yeah, I'll bet that's what it is."

"Yeah." He said.

"Yeah?" She asked.

"Yeah." He confirmed. "Let's keep going."

They walked a few yards further and Felicity stopped.

"There's just one thing I'm not clear about."

"What's that?"

"What were you doing in the middle of the road when I came into town that first night?"

"I wasn't ever on the road that night."

"Yes, you were, out on the highway, I nearly ran you over and you took off into the trees."

Greg took Felicity's hand and held onto it tightly.

"Felicity, I was in town and I drove my truck home. I never once stepped foot onto the road that night."

The End.

About the Author

Valerie Loveless is also the author of Enduring Promises of the Heart, Unbroken Promises of the Heart and children's book: Anabel Loves Babies. My Bigfoot Boyfriend started out as an April Fool's joke in 2019, when she posted a fake cover and blurb about it on her blog as a new book release. Not thinking it could ever become an actual story, Valerie forgot about it until one day the main plotline popped into her head. She knew she had to make it reality and in one weekend the first draft was done. Valerie lives in Utah with her three kids, two chihuahuas and her incredibly supportive husband who thinks chicks who write about pirates, mermaids and bigfoots are pretty hot.

www.valerieloveless.info

Other Books by Valerie Loveless:

Enduring Promises of the Heart

The year is 1887, and the small community of Pleasant View is abuzz over Penelope Pottifer's serialized romances in the local paper. Since the release of the first volume, the thrilling story has captured the hearts and minds of the entire town— and several towns over!
Each successive edition of the Pleasant View Gazette spins a breathtaking tale of kidnappers, pirates, and forbidden love. Between volumes, however, Pleasant View resident Mary Clarence, the story's toughest critic, hears a rumor that Penelope Pottifer is not, in fact, the author's real name. Determined to uncover the mystery, Mary drags her friend Elizabeth Black into a hunt for the elusive author's true identity. But fiction and reality seem to entwine when along the way, Mary and Liz discover unexpected truths, exciting adventures, and dramatic romances of their own.

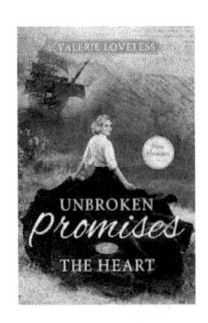

Unbroken Promises of the Heart

Liz and Mary Scheme to make Mary's dream of owning a hat shop come true, they are unaware that their husbands, Michael and Peter are scheming behind their backs to try to realize a dream of theirs that the girls do not discover until late in the story. Harriet, Liz's sister, has come home and has eyes for the mysterious Isaac all the while being pursued by the quirky revered Lyons. Harriet, with the help of her famous sister, gets a job editing at the Gazette but the pudgy, foolish son of the owner, continually makes her job awkward are difficult. He is determined to undermine her position and make her his wife. Liz struggles with being a newlywed, being "With Child" and keeping up on her writing, Mary and her sister Harriet attempt to help her navigate this difficult time as her Peter seems to be preoccupied. In the meantime, the gazette featurette progresses with the botched wedding of Lavender and John by the miraculously undead pirate, Morose. Morose claims to have been rescued by a mermaid. Morose bestows a precious gift to Lavender and then she uncharacteristically runs off with him. John has to travel the world to discover the reason his true love has left him for Morose with the help of Paully and his reformed daughter Nan Fey.

CPSIA information can be obtained
at www.ICGtesting.com
Printed in the USA
BVHW040348060821
613815BV00022B/314